T0063135

ISLANDS OF LOVE

ISLANDS OF LOVE

CHRISTINE TAN SEON RHIM

PARTRIDGE
A Penguin Random House Company

To order additional copies of this book, contact
Toll Free 800 101 2657 (Singapore)
Toll Free 1 800 81 7340 (Malaysia)
orders.singapore@partridgepublishing.com

www.partridgepublishing.com/singapore

CONTENTS

Chp 1

◆

A Painful Loss

At 6.30pm, Young-tae had finished work, he tidied up his workstation and went to his manager's office.

"Mr Kim, I'm leaving the office, please call me if you need me." Young-tae was standing at the door of his manager's office.

His superior was going through some document, he lifted his head briefly and nodded his approval with a smile. Usually Young-tae would finish his work after 7.30pm and leave office after his manager, but today he had a private tuition appointment, so he left early. He had been working in HyungDai Bank in Seoul since he graduated from college, and now he was a senior financial executive with the bank. At the age of 35, he considered himself lucky to have climbed the corporate ladder truly based on his hard work and dedication.

As he left the office building, he bought a sandwich from a nearby bakery shop before he walked to the subway station. As he got off the train, he ate his sandwich while on the way to his student's house. After walking for about

10 minutes, he came to the gate of a mansion, and pressed the doorbell. A middle-aged domestic helper came to open the gate for him. He thanked the helper and went into the mansion.

"This behaviour of yours is unacceptable! You failed your test and you were out watching movie with your boyfriend! Are you trying to become a school dropout?" The voice of the owner of the house, Mr Choi, was getting louder as Young-tae approached the front door of the mansion.

"You are a student, you must study hard, or else you will not achieve any success in future. How do you build your self-confidence as a person? That is from your good result and good attitude toward your school work and toward the people around you. If you can't even pass a simple test, would you feel good? Surely you won't feel good, are you going to carry that feeling for the rest of your life?" Mr Choi gave a dressing down to her teenage daughter, but he did not compare her with her elder sister and brother, who did well in school without much supervision, and were now managing the family businesses, as it might make Min-hye, his youngest daughter, more defiant.

"You are to come home straight after school from now till the year-end examination!" Mr Choi concluded his speech by forbidding his youngest daughter to engage in any activity outside school.

When Young-tae entered the living room, Mr Choi and Mrs Choi were sitting on the sofa, while Min-hye, Young-tae's tuition student, was kneeling on the marble floor next to the sofa.

"Mr Joo, you are here. I'll get the helper to serve dinner now." Mrs Choi was pleased to see Young-tae, though rather embarrassed, as Young-tae might be their only hope to improve their daughter's grades.

"Good evening Mr Choi, Mrs Choi. Oh, I've just had a sandwich, please don't prepare dinner for me." Young-tae declined the dinner treat politely.

"Mr Joo, me and my husband are going out for dinner, please dine with Min-hye, she has not taken dinner yet." Appealed Mrs Choi sincerely.

"All right then, thank you." Replied Young-tae, then he went to the study room to put his briefcase and coat. They had dinner in the dining room. Dinner was rather simple, which included rice, noodles, stir-fried eggs, pickled vegetables, and some barbecue meat.

After dinner, Young-tae and Min-hye was in the study room getting ready for the Mathematics tuition. Min-hye was looking depressed, she felt especially embarrassed as her tutor had witnessed the dressing down and her kneeling on the floor. Her mouth was tightly shut and her brooding face was turning the other way.

"Min-hye, not ready for the lesson?" Young-tae thought he should try to get the lesson going. "You know a lot of school dropouts are intelligent people? I would be sad if a smart girl like you would give up your studies." Young-tae tried to motivate and coax Min-hye back to her studies, at the same time chose his words carefully so as not to upset her further.

Much to her dismay, Min-hye's activities were limited within the school, which means she would not have a chance to meet her boyfriend as her boyfriend was from another school. Her father had instructed the driver to send her to school and pick her up after school. She was occupied with these thoughts and did not reply her tutor.

"Hmm...I wonder..., would your parents replace me with another tutor if your grades don't improve?" Young-tae tried again to communicate with her, at the same time to find out whether Min-hye was dissatisfied with him as her tutor.

"I'm sorry, please continue to coach me. Teacher, you saw and heard what happened earlier on, I'm really not in the mood to study." Min-hye did not think there was a need to get another tutor. She began to communicate with Young-tae and sought his understanding of her situation.

"Well then, hmm..." Young-tae was glad Min-hye's attitude had changed to be more positive. "Today we'll just discuss the chapters and the requirements for the examination." Said Young-tae.

The atmosphere in the study room had become more relaxed, Young-tae would sometimes give a pat on Min-hye's shoulder to console and encourage her. Looking at Min-hye doing homework, he felt a tint of sadness in his body, as the memories of an unfortunate event flashed before him.

It was a windy afternoon, Young-tae and Eun-ja were on their way home after school. They were both 16 years old and were in love. Wearing school uniforms, with school bags on their back, they were chatting and teasing each other along the road. They would pass by a row of trees and climb onto one of them. The wind was getting rather harsh that day, but it did not bother them.

All they did was climbed onto a sturdy tree branch, sat on it and enjoyed the feeling of floating in the air for a couple of minutes. Little did they know, that afternoon, a small scale hurricane was looming. Moments after they sat on the tree branch they used to patronize, lightning flashed and thunder rumbled, cracking the greenish sky. In a second, a howling wind swept through the area, swinging trees left and right and splitting tree branches. Some trees were uprooted and fell onto the road.

Young-tae and Eun-ja were terrified by the menacing wind, but before they could descend to the ground, the tree branch they were on was torn off from the tree trunk. While scrambling to grab other tree branches, they were both swept off balance by the ferocious storm, they lost their footing and fell three metres below onto the riverbank.

"Help me, Young-tae..." That was the last time Young-tae heard Eun-ja's voice, he could not do anything as his head was hurt as he fell on the rough ground and he had soon lost consciousness. The riverbank was lined with stones and pebbles, both of them were injured from falling hard on the ground. They were lying there motionless, a pool of blood emerged from the back of Eun-ja's head and flew into the river, creating a stream of red water in the river.

The hurricane had stopped rampaging the outlaying suburb and serenity had resumed. More than one hour had past, the sun was setting, but both of them were still lying unconscious on the riverbank.

"Young-tae...Young-tae..." Young Tae's worried parents came to look for him as their son would usually come home in the late afternoon before sunset. The voices had awakened Young-tae, he felt a sharp pain in his head, but was able to move his body and sit upright. He could recognize his parents' voices.

"Eun-ja...Eun-ja..." When he saw Eun-ja lying nearby, he rushed over and tried to wake her up, but his effort was futile.

"Mom, dad, I'm down here, come and help Eun-ja!" He shouted for his parents. He was terrified when he saw Eun-ja was losing a lot of blood, and started crying uncontrollably as he shook Eun-ja's lifeless body.

Young-tae's father followed his son's voice and hurried down to the riverbank, his wife was behind him. When he saw Eun-ja, he quickly put his fingers on her nose to feel her breathing, then he pressed his right palm on her chest to feel for her heartbeat. The body was cold, there was no breathing, no heartbeat.

He dreaded to tell Young-tae his findings, but it was not right to hide it from him, so he said, "Young-tae, be strong, I'm afraid Eun-ja has left us."

Young-tae's mind went blank when he heard that, he trembled and cried, "No…...! Dad, please save her…!" He could not accept the fact that Eun-ja was dead, he was crying and pestering his father to save Eun-ja. His father slowly turned Eun-ja's head, and found a punctured hole at the back of her head. He used his towel to wrap around Eun-ja's head, trying to stop any further bleeding.

"How is she?" Asked Young-tae's mother anxiously. Her husband did not answer her as he knew Eun-ja was dead, so he lifted her cold body and carried her to the main road. Young-tae and his mother followed close behind, waving at passing by vehicles, hoping to get a ride to the local hospital. A kind-hearted driver stopped his vehicle and sent them to the hospital.

The doctor who tried to revive Eun-ja came out of the emergency room, and told them Eun-ja passed away about an hour ago due to profuse blood lost. Young-tae burst into a loud cry and slumped to the floor upon hearing the announcement.

"Teacher...Teacher...care to have some fruits?" The domestic helper had brought some cut fruits to the study room, Min-hye placed the fruits in front of Young-tae, who was absorbed in his own recollection, to get his attention.

"Okay..." Young-tae was pulled back from his flashback by Min-hye's voice, he was looking rather dispirited. Eun-ja's death was devastatingly painful to him, his heart was torn into pieces every time he had these flashbacks.

"Teacher, is something bothering you?" Min-hye noticed the gloomy look on her tutor.

"I'm fine, let's carry on with the lesson." Young-tae collected his composure and went through Min-hye's homework with her.

Love for the Islands

In the past few years, Young-tae would visit an island once or twice a month for outdoor painting, as well as to escape the hustle and bustle of the city life. It was 7am on a Saturday morning, while packing his painting equipment into his haversack, his mobile phone rang.

"Hi dear, have you taken breakfast? Which island are you visiting today?" It was his girlfriend Rui-a.

Rui-a was Eun-ja's younger cousin, they were living in the same suburban area. She and her family were close to Young-tae since Eun-ja passed away. When Young-tae did his college course in Seoul, Rui-a, her mother and a younger sister also moved to Seoul as Rui-a was studying her design courses in Seoul.

"Hey, you are up early today. I'll be going to Nami Island, can you join me today?" Young-tae would love Rui-a to spend some time on the island with him. He felt she had been working too hard.

"I'm sorry, I brought some work home to do, I need to get them done before Monday. I miss you, how I wish I could go with you." Replied Rui-a.

Being an architect, Rui-a had endless meetings to attend and multiple deadlines to meet, sometimes she had to bring clients out for dinners after working hours, and had been habitually working over the weekends. To her, spending a day or two on an island was a luxury she could not afford.

"I miss you too, try to take more rest, don't spend all your time working on a weekend. Love you." Young-tae replied with a loving greeting, as it was a nice and warm gesture for his girlfriend to call early in the morning.

"Love you too. Stay safe, remember to take your breakfast, call me when you are back." Replied Rui-a, she was used to not able to find time to accompany him on his painting trips.

Young-tae loved to visit Nami Island during Autumn, as he could capture the splendour of the colourful landscape in his paintings. That morning, he bought a ferry ticket and entrance ticket to Nami Island from the ferry wharf, bought some snacks for breakfast, boarded a ferry and arrived at the island around 9.30am.

He walked around the island in a leisurely pace, breathing in fresh air and strolling along the paths lined with tall trees which are now full of orange, red and yellow leaves. As usual, he would take some pictures, and look for a spot away from the tourists, to set up his easel.

While painting, he would consciously immerse himself in nature. He would imagine himself as falling leaves, dancing with the wind and landing softly onto the ground. Sometimes he was the trickling water, streaming on top of rocks and pebbles, flowing incessantly in the river. And sometimes he was a tall pine tree, rustling his tree branches and leaves tirelessly in the wind.

The islands were ideal places to create such absolute harmony between him and nature, which allowed him to thoroughly relax his mind and body.

Young-tae took up painting also to keep him occupied. Most of the time he used acrylic paints when he was painting outdoor as these paints are fast-drying, they are easier to manage. He mainly painted landscapes, focusing less on portraits, or abstract, etc. Painting was a therapeutic hobby from the beginning, there was no plans, no ambition, or no timeline to become a professional painter. Perhaps such a disposition was the reason why he was still an amateur painter after he had been painting for several years

Gradually, the regular trips he took to the islands have become a routine for him to attain peace of mind outside his earthly responsibilities. When he totally immersed himself in nature, he was painting in the most carefree ways. He painted the same kind of scenery, overtime he would improve on his painting skill, mixing the colours to be as similar as the real subjects, interchanging smooth sketches with rugged strokes, and painting at the best time when the landscapes were most breathtaking, etc.

Without pressuring himself, years of such constant effort has come to fruition. The landscapes he painted have become more lifelike, the paintings are in vivid colours, with rich textures, and reflecting the rugged nature and the serenity of the landscapes in perfection. In short, the islands have nurtured him into a landscape painter with masterly skills.

That day, Young-tae was painting the paths which lined with rows of tall trees with colourful leaves. He stood in front of his easel and canvas, closed his eyes and felt the morning scent. The cool breeze on the island was whispering in his ears, ruffling his shirt and caressing his body. Perhaps he was the morning breeze, brushing every tall tree, swaying them slightly. He would play with the falling leaves, tossing them one by one, and watching them somersaulting in the air. Then he would pass by the forest and mountain, cruising above the ocean, and swishing through every corner of the island.

Hours have passed, the painting was not completed yet, but he had to stop painting as the sun was setting. He would usually bring back the unfinished works and continue to work on them at his apartment. So he waited for the paint to dry on the canvas, kept his paints and brushes, folded the easel, then carried his belongings and left the island.

The next day, he completed his painting in his apartment in the late afternoon, and visited Rui-a and her family in the evening.

"Auntie, good evening, how have you been?" Young-tae greeted Mdm Shim, who was sitting in the living room sofa watching TV, as he entered their house.

"Young-tae is here. Rui-a, Joo-a, Young-tae is here, let's have dinner." Mdm Shim, Rui-a's mother, was getting ready to serve dinner. Mdm Shim had no doubt that Young-tae would be her future son-in-law. Not only because she had known Young-tae for more than twenty years, but also because Young-tae was a responsible person, he had a stable job, steady income, and led a decent lifestyle.

"Brother, I can't solve some mathematical problems, please teach me later, okay?" Joo-a came out from her room, holding and swinging Young-tae's arm, pestering him to help solve her mathematical problems.

"Sure, no problem, Joo-a, let's have dinner first." Young-tae put his hand around Joo-a's shoulder, they then took their seats at the dining table.

Joo-a, Rui-a's younger sister, looked up to Young-tae as a role-model. Young-tae was good in his studies, and was always warm and caring toward her. She was a cheerful and energetic teenager, now studying in a high school in Seoul. She loved sports, and was an active member of her school's cheerleading team.

"Hi dear, you are here, how's the trip to Nami Island?" Rui-a came out from the study room and sat next to Young-tae.

"It was good, I have a good time. How's your work?" Young-tae asked.

"I've finally got it done, what a relief." Rui-a looked at Young-tae, then she held his hand. Young-tae smiled at her and said, "That's good, but you looked tired."

"I'll go to bed early tonight, don't worry." Replied Rui-a, and she laid her head on his shoulder for a short while.

"Young-tae, it's such a good thing to do, I mean, going to islands regularly and spending hours there, you could really relax while you are painting." Even though Mdm Shim thought Young-tae had spent quite a lot of time on island trips, but she felt it was good for him to have a healthy hobby. Moreover, Rui-a was always busy with work, she could not blame Young-tae for not spending enough time with her daughter.

"Yes, Auntie. I'm still very interested in painting on the islands. It helps to relax my mind and body." Replied Young-tae.

"Brother, can I join you the next time you go on an island trip?" Joo-a was interested as well, pestering Young-tae to let her join him on an island trip.

"All right, but you'll feel bored very soon because I'm always painting, I don't really go sightseeing. Anyway, focus on your study for the time being, plan the trips after your examination, okay?" Said Young-tae.

"Mom, you know, Young-tae's painting skills are getting better nowadays, his works are like masterpieces, is that right, Young-tae?" Rui-a was proud of her boyfriend's progress in painting.

"Really, I don't know about paintings, can you show me some of your works during your next visit?" Mdm Shim was eager to see Young-tae's works since her daughter gave such a positive evaluation of his works.

"All right, Auntie. There is still room for improvement in terms of my painting skills, I can't consider myself a master." Young-tae was delighted with Rui-a's comment, but he was humble, and would not flatter himself.

"I'm serious, mom, Young-tae can be a famous painter soon. I'm looking out for an opportunity to get his works displayed in exhibitions." Rui-a sounded really enthusiastic about getting Young-tae's works exhibited.

"You have a busy schedule, where do you find time to do this for me?" Young-tae was surprised to hear such a proposition, at the same time contemplating its possibility.

"I came across some exhibition organizers while working on some projects, sometimes we exchanged ideas on interior decoration, sculptures, and art works, etc. I'll get more information about the exhibitions, are you against the idea?" Rui-a was curious about how Young-tae would feel about having his works exhibited for sale.

"Of course not, I'm worried you would overwork yourself on top of your busy schedule, I just don't want you to be too tired." Young-tae had felt Rui-a had been working too hard. On the other hand, he did not feel his works are masterpieces, but it would be rather exciting to have his paintings exhibited.

"All right then. Don't worry, it won't take up too much of my time." Rui-a gave her assurance, and was determined to explore such opportunities for Young-tae.

"Brother, come and help me with my mathematical problems." After dinner, they chatted in the living room for a while, and Joo-a reminded Young-tae to help her out.

"Let's see what's troubling you." Young-tae went to the study room with Joo-a.

"Joo-a, Young-tae got to wake up early tomorrow morning for his work, try not to take up too much of his time." Mdm Shim reminded her younger daughter.

"Okay, mom." Replied Joo-a from the study room.

Kept the Doctor Away

It was a Friday evening, Young-tae was meeting someone for a drink in a pub. He entered the bar, perhaps he was early, he could not find the familiar face he was supposed to meet, as such, he went to the bar counter and ordered a beer.

"Hey, Young-tae." A man in his 30's entered the pub, he joined Young-tae at the bar counter as soon as he spotted him.

"Dr Kang, long time no see." Young-tae greeted Dr Kang Woo-hyun, a psychiatrist whom he sought consultation with in the past.

"It's been two years since we last met, how have you been?" Dr Kang was the one who rang Young-tae up for this meeting. After Young-tae completed a series of therapy sessions conducted by Dr Kang, they did not contact each other. Dr Kang called him up for a meeting as he was concerned how Young-tae had been doing without therapy.

"So you are married?" Young-tae noticed a wedding band on Dr Kang's ring finger.

"Well, I got married last year. How about you?" Dr Kang knew Rui-a as well, thought they might be married too.

"I've not planned about it, I guess it's about time for me to get married as well. Can't make Rui-a wait forever, right?" Young-tae's cynical remark was directed at himself, as he felt a sense of contrition since marriage was not on his mind at that moment, even though he was old enough, and was financially stable.

"I was surprised to receive your call, but it's really good to hear from you again." Young-tae was thinking Dr Kang probably wanted him to go back for some more therapy sessions, which he would try hard to avoid should Dr Kang bring up the issue.

"It's good to see you again, really, you look fine to me, I mean you look more relaxed and less tensed. I was thinking maybe you could come back for evaluative sessions, I would like to assess if there are any changes on you after your last therapy sessions." Dr Kang deemed the evaluative sessions as necessary to gauge whether Young-tae needed any further psychological treatment.

"I see...Well, I guess I'm about the same with or without therapy. After I completed the last session with you, I went through the daily routines in the same manner, doing the same work, and conducting the same hobby, I actually felt better and healthier. I mean, I felt as if I've fully recovered from a sickness." Going back for therapy sessions sounded rather dreary for Young-tae, as that means he was not 'out of the woods' yet.

"So, how's your island trips, are you still visiting the islands regularly?" Dr Kang switched topic as he sensed some dismal in Young-tae's reply.

"I love painting on the islands, yes, I've been visiting them regularly, at least once or twice a month." Replied Young-tae, he was still contemplating whether to resume the therapy sessions.

"That's great. I'm truly glad that the relaxing techniques have loosened you up quite a bit. Well done!" Encouraged Dr Kang. He knew Young-tae had worked for years to achieve a frame of mind that was truly calm and relax, but he felt some elements were still missing, and it was his duty to study his condition closely so as to build a healthier psyche for Young-tae.

"Here, this is my name card, come and see me sometime next month, I'll get the staff in the clinic to fix an appointment for you. Don't worry, it's just some evaluative sessions." Said Dr Kang condescendingly, and swiftly passed his name card to Young-tae.

"Umm..." Young-tae was at a loss for words, before he could turn down Dr Kang's proposition, he was holding Dr Kang's name card.

"All right then, let's get out of this place." Dr Kang did not wait for Young-tae to reply, he went to the cashier counter and settled the bill.

Chp 2

◆

An Accident in the Park

Joo-a was in a national school cheerleading competition on this Saturday morning. Inside the stadium, the event was progressing like a rock concert, waves of rhythmic cheers and thundering applauses erupting every now and then. The boisterous atmosphere would elevate to the highest point whenever there was an excellent performance, such as a performer had somersaulted in the air and then landed perfectly with the help of her teammates. Rui-a and Young-tae were at the audience hall, totally captivated by the performances of the competition. When Joo-a's team was performing, they were all excited, clapping their hands and cheering slogans as loud as they could with her school's supporters.

After the competition, Rui-a had to attend a seminar organized by her company in Jeju Island. Young-tae and Joo-a were sending her to the airport.

"Joo-a, mom would be away for a few days, later you dine out with Young-tae. I'll take a cab back tomorrow afternoon." Said Joo-a while they were on the way to the airport.

"Yes, sis, can I go cycling with brother before dinner?" Joo-a asked her sister, she dreaded the idea of going home in the afternoon, as she would have to be alone by herself in the house.

"All right, just be careful. Don't forget to do your homework after dinner. Young-tae, could you bring her to the park later?" Rui-a asked Young-tae, she thought it would be good for them to engage in some outdoor activities.

"Sure, no problem. Joo-a, we'll go cycling at the park, after that I'll treat you to dinner." Young-tae replied, then he asked Rui-a, "Why not let me fetch you at the airport tomorrow?"

"I'll be fine. You take a good rest at home." Rui-a thought she too needed a good rest after the trip.

"All right then, have a safe trip. Should we go for a quick bite at the airport now?" Asked Young-tae.

"That's great, let's go to the fast food restaurant before I board the plane." Said Rui-a.

After sending off Rui-a, Young-tae and Joo-a went to a park with cycling paths. They rented two bicycles from a bicycle rental store for an hour's ride.

"Joo-a, don't go too fast, ride safely to avoid accidents, ok?" Young-tae reminded Joo-a.

"Yes, brother…I'll be careful." Joo-a was in good spirit, she was happy to have a chance to come cycling, especially when Young-tae was accompanying her. She felt safe and protected.

Young-tae followed closely behind Joo-a, he would raise his voice to ask her to slow down if she went too fast, or if he thought there were possible dangers ahead. The afternoon breeze was cooling and refreshing, Young-tae was glad he got a chance to do some exercise in the park as well.

After cycling for ten minutes, Young-tae became anxious when Joo-a suddenly disappeared from his vision as he came to a curving path. He quickened his cycling pace to look for her, but she was nowhere in sight, then he heard a cry beyond the bushes and saw her bicycle lying on the slope. He thought some mishaps must have happened to Joo-a, he quickly laid his bicycle near the bushes and hurried down the slope.

"Ahh…ahh…brother.." Joo-a was moaning at the foot of the slope. She was panic when a speeding skateboarder almost crashed into her bike. She lost control of her bike, wiggled her way through the bushes and tumbled down the slope.

"Joo-a, are you all right…what happened…are you hurt?" Young-tae was petrified when he saw Joo-a lying on the ground. The scene which Eun-ja lost her life after they fell from the tree flashed in front of his eyes. His deepest fear had resurfaced, his heart was racing fast, and cold sweat trickled down his face.

"Joo-a…are you okay?" Young-tae examined her hands and legs, and found some bruises on her arms and elbows.

"Brother, my elbows hurt..my back is painful.." Joo-a had suffered some pain in her elbows and at the back of her body.

"I'm sorry, I shouldn't have brought you here to cycle…" A distressed Young-tae started to apologize. He held her closely and massaged her back and arms.

"Sorry, Joo-a, it's entirely my fault that you are injured, we should not have come cycling..." Slipping into a state of self-reproach, Young-tae kept mumbling that it was his mistake for her mishap.

Perhaps Joo-a was mesmerized by the close proximity of Young-tae's body, the person whom she admired and adored in her adolescent years. She felt a strong chemical attraction for him under his utmost care and protection. She hugged him closely, displaying her affection. And perhaps Young-tae's fear of losing Joo-a thwarted his judgement, he could not let go of her body. In a way, it was as though he was holding Eun-ja's body, and now Eun-ja was alive. He was soaking in the solace of such surreal belief. Bedazzled in their own fantasies, they began to make out in the open, at the foot of the slope.

About half an hour later, they returned the bicycles to the rental store and left the park, and went to a nearby restaurant for dinner. The restaurant was filled with chattering noise, but Young-tae and Joo-a took their dinner in silence. Sitting opposite and facing each other was awkward, they did not make any conversation until they were in the car.

"I'll confess to your sister when she comes back tomorrow, let me talk to her." Young-tae had decided a confession should take place as soon as Rui-a returned from Jeju Island.

"If you tell sis, mom will get to know and she'll chase me out of the house. If that happens, where am I supposed to go?" Joo-a pondered over the consequences.

"I'll take full responsibility...I'll take care of you and protect you, you can come live with me." Young-tae had no idea what to do other than owning up to Rui-a even though he knew Rui-a would be devastated upon hearing the affair. At that instant, he was intensely disgusted by himself for not being able to control his desire.

"I can't leave my mom and sis, I can't imagine any changes in my life…can't let them know, I would be in deep trouble." Joo-a thought owning up would invite a disastrous outcome.

"Don't worry, I'll handle everything." Young-tae insisted on telling the truth and accepting whatever consequences there might be.

"No! Can't you keep a secret? It's not wise to create a havoc and turn everyone's life upside down just because of one insignificant incident!" Joo-a was in a state of agitation, she raised her voice to put her message across loud and clear. However, she was ashamed of herself as she had betrayed her sister's love and care for her in the past years.

"I…all right…let's leave it that way. I'm truly sorry…I was carried away in the park this afternoon, it won't happen again." An apologetic Young-tae finally gave in to Joo-a to pacify her.

Joo-a's heart was broken when she heard 'it won't happen again', as it would suggest that their intimate affair was engaged in a moment of folly, he was not in love with her, and that he had no intention of developing a real relationship with her. The thought of being taken advantage of crossed her mind, it was unsettling, she took a deep breath, and tried to maintain a calm composure. The only thing she could do at that time was to forget about the whole incident to save her from further heartaches and misery.

Marriage Ritual for Eun-ja

Several gloomy days had passed, Young-tae was feeling suffocated no matter what he did and where he went. He decided to go camping on Jungdo Island over the weekend to breathe in some fresh air and clear his mind. That Saturday morning, he packed some camping stuff into his haversack, and brought along his painting equipment for the trip.

It was a peaceful day on Jungdo Island, there was not too many tourists as it had been raining in the morning. Young-tae arrived on the island in the late morning, he began hiking along a mountain trail to reach the peak where he could enjoy the panoramic view of the Soyang lake. He took some pictures and then ventured to another area to view a waterfall. The sky had started to drizzle for a while, if it rained he would need a shelter, so he went to the camping ground to rent a tent, thinking he could continue with the hiking later, or the next day.

The rain had started to fall heavily shortly after Young-tae set up his tent. Sitting in his tent, the rain was pouring ceaselessly. While listening to the noisy thuds on his tent, memories of past events filled his mind.

That morning, Eun-ja's body, wrapped in pure white hanbok, was sent back to her parents' house. A white-coloured makeshift tent was erected next to their house. Her parents had also set up an altar with Eun-ja's picture, long candles and food for prayers. A ritual to be conducted by a female shaman would take place before her body was laid down in the coffin. Eun-ja's family and relatives were in mourning attire, sitting near one side of the altar. Eun-ja's mother was crying most of the time, sometimes she would call Eun-ja's name, sometimes she would stay silent when she was tired of crying. Friends and neighbours sat near the family and relatives, they too were heartbroken that Eun-ja had died at such a young age.

Eun-ja's body was rested on a platform behind the altar. The female shaman, holding a golden scepter in one hand and a paper fan in another, clothed in white and red traditional shaman costume, started the ritual for the deceased with chanting and some dance movements.

An hour had past, Young-tae, wearing an all-white coloured hanbok, was summoned by the shaman to lie down next to Eun-ja's body. Another ritual would follow, which was agreed by Eun-ja's parents, Young-tae's parents, as well as Young-tae himself, that was to conduct a spiritual marriage between Eun-ja and Young-tae, so that Eun-ja would not be lonely in heaven, she would be accompanied by Young-tae's spirit.

The shaman was seen holding a white silky sash, raising it high up with both hands and praying to heaven, a few minutes later, she turned to face the altar and started chanting. She was chanting while she approached Young-tae and Eun-ja's body, then she wrapped Eun-ja's right hand in a circular movement with one end of the sash and did the same movement to Young-tae's left hand with the other end of the sash.

After the bonding between the 'bride and groom' was completed, the shaman then proceeded to the front of the altar and started a dance with much vigour, symbolizing the celebration of a holy matrimony.

During the 'marriage ritual', family members and relatives, friends and neighbours, were observing their silence, they were praying for a good journey to heaven for the deceased. Such a ritual could assuage the grief of those left behind. Especially Eun-ja's mother, she had stopped weeping and started to talk to the people who came to convey their heartfelt condolences. The ritual had brought a sense of calmness to Young-tae's mind, he was in a better spirit, and began to help out with chores to be done for the ritual.

Young-tae was lying down in the tent, turning one way or the other once in a while. He could only stay inside the tent as the rain was still pouring.

"Eun-ja, are you crying? I receive your message from the rain…please don't cry…when you left me so suddenly.…I'm still heartbroken and devastated…." Young-tae started to mumble to himself in the tent.

"I'm sorry for climbing the tree with you, and I'm sorry for being alive when you are dead…Our marriage was divine, which had helped me survived up till now…now I've Rui-a, your younger cousin, whom I should marry soon…" Young-tae was talking instinctively and casually.

"Eun-ja, I'm living a proper life, but my heart is heavy, like the pouring rain…I kept myself busy, working, giving tuition and painting on islands…sometimes I see you in the sky, smiling at me.…It was the happiest thing that have happened to me since you left…I was blessed that you are watching over me…at times, I felt like rising to the sky to meet you…but that was just a thought…" Young-tae muttered on, as though Eun-ja was lying next to him.

"Eun-ja, sometimes I feel like walking into the ocean to look for you…or hiking in the forest hoping to meet you by chance…I know these are impractical thoughts…but what am I supposed to do…I can't see you and hold you anymore…" Young-tae's mind was drifting to a dreamlike state.

"Eun-ja…what to do with Rui-a…I should marry her… but how should I treat her…she is capable, honest, and warm…she is filial and responsible, and loyal to me….how do I make her happy when we get married…" Young-tae voiced out his concern, he was expecting some answers from Eun-ja's spirit, perhaps in his dream.

The next morning, Young-tae woke up coughing and sneezing, he was shivering as his body was cold. Then he remembered the night before, he fell asleep without putting on his down jacket. Feeling feverish from the cold and weak from hunger, he packed his stuff, dismantled the tent and returned it to the rental store.

Young-tae took his breakfast at the pier harbour after he got off the ferry, after that he headed back to Seoul. His fever did not subside when he returned to his apartment, so he took some herbal medicine as remedy and went to bed.

On Monday morning, he woke up feeling worse, his head was heavy and his body was aching. He called his manager in the office that he was down with a flu, and he went to see a doctor for some medication and a medical certificate.

Mdm Shim was at his apartment to take care of him when Rui-a told her Young-tae was sick. Since morning, she put his laundry into the washer, mopped the floor, and cleaned the furniture. Mdm Shim treated Young-tae like her own son, looking after him when he fell ill was an innate responsibility.

In the afternoon, Joo-a went to the apartment to visit Young-tae when school was over for the day.

"Brother, are you better now?" Joo-a was sitting by his bed, looking rather worried.

"Joo-a, I'm sorry, that day we shouldn't go cycling at the park, it's my fault that you fell and injured yourself." Young-tae, apologized to Joo-a once again, about their intimate affair in the park. He could not mention it out loud as Mdm Shim was in the apartment.

"I'm fine now, I was panic when I saw the skateboarder speeding towards me, I lost control of the bike instantly. It's not your fault." Said Joo-a, she knew Young-tae meant to apologize for their intimate affair in the park.

Joo-a held his hands and showed that she had put the incident behind her. It was a great relief for Young-tae as he and Joo-a could still maintain a congenial relationship.

"Young-tae, there were only some bruises on her elbows, don't think about it anymore. I've cooked some porridge, take your lunch and you can take your medication." Said Mdm Shim, she then went to the kitchen and ladled the porridge to a bowl and brought it for Young-tae.

"Brother, where is your medication? I'll get it for you." Joo-a was back to her cheerful ways, volunteering to get Young-tae's medication for him.

In the evening, when Rui-a finished her work at the office, she came to see Young-tae in his apartment.

"Mom, sister is here." Joo-a opened the door for her, she was doing her homework at the dining table.

Rui-a went to see Young-tae in his bedroom. Mdm Shim was preparing dinner at the kitchenette.

"Are you feeling better? You look pale." Rui-a held his hand and touched his forehead to feel for his temperature.

"I'm better after taking the medication, how are you today?" Young-tae was glad to see Rui-a, her presence was comforting to him.

"Just a bit tired. Did you bring your down jacket with you when you go camping?" Rui-a felt it was partly her fault, because if she went camping with Young-tae, he might not have fallen sick.

"I brought the jacket but when I fell asleep I did not put it on. It's not a big deal, I'll recover real soon." Replied Young-tae, he was glad to see his girlfriend showering her love on him, and he caressed her arm tenderly.

"You won't fall sick if I were with you, I'm sorry, I should spend more time with you. Should I keep you company tonight?" Said Rui-a, thinking she should do something to make it up to him, and that would make Young-tae feel better.

"It's just a flu, stop worrying. Go back early to get some good rest." Said Young-tae, even though he would love her to stay, but he knew she needed a good sleep to wake up early for work the next morning.

"Rui-a, Young-tae, dinner is ready." Mdm Shim called them for dinner. Rui-a helped Young-tae get out of bed, she put Young-tae's hand over her shoulder and they walked slowly to the dining table.

"Young-tae, I need to show your paintings to an art gallery manager, can we discuss about this after dinner?"

Rui-a had enquired about an opportunity to showcase Young-tae's paintings.

"All right, we'll do that later." Young-tae replied with a tender smile.

After dinner, they were at the study room, where Young-tae kept his paintings. He explained to them where he painted the landscapes, what was the season, and so on. They exchanged views and picked some paintings for Rui-a to send for framing before showing them to the manager.

A Motivated Student

This was a typical day where Young-tae knocked off early from work for his tuition appointment. When he arrived at the front door of the Choi mansion, Min-hye was sitting in the living room waiting for him.

"Good evening, teacher." Min-hye greeted Young-tae as she carried his briefcase and coat to the study room. She returned in an instant to accompany him to the dining table.

"I see you are in good spirit today, that's good." Observed Young-tae, as they proceeded to the dining table.

"Teacher, my mom said to make sure you take dinner before the tuition. Please feel at ease, and don't stand on ceremony, okay? Auntie, please give us two bowls of rice." Min-hye called for the domestic helper to serve dinner.

"Please send my regards to your parents, and tell them I really appreciate their kindness for treating me to dinner every time I'm here." A modest Young-tae expressed his gratitude.

"I'll tell mom when she comes back. My mom and dad went out for a walk in the neighbourhood." Min-hye was supposed to wait for her tutor to dine with him.

"Tell me why you are in such a good mood today." Young-tae was delighted to see a change in Min-hye's attitude, as she was crestfallen in the past few weeks when her parents prohibited her from engaging in any activities outside school hours.

"My dad allowed me to go out on Saturdays because I get better grades in my recent tests." A cheery Min-hye revealed the reason.

"That's great, well done!" Young-tae was pleased to see Min-hye had put in effort in improving her grades, he showed his encouragement by patting her shoulder slightly.

After dinner, they were in the study room, getting ready to begin their lessons. Min-hye brought out a file and pulled out her mathematics test paper, the score was 78. Then she showed Young-tae her language and science test papers, the scores were all above 75.

"Teacher, see my results, I've improved a lot." Min-hye's face was beaming with confidence.

"Wow, that's truly remarkable. I see your parents are right to make you stay at home to study." Teased Young-tae, he was truly pleased to see Min-hye's improvement.

"My mom said I couldn't achieve these results without your help." It seemed her parents had given kudos to Young-tae for their daughter's fine performance.

"That's not true, you earned these grades through hard work, you should be proud of yourself." Young-tae thought Min-hye should get all the merits for her hard work.

"Teacher, I can't achieve these good grades without your encouragement and patience. Thank you."

Young-tae was amazed to see such a transformation in his student. Not only her grades had improved, she had also become more matured and sensible.

During the lesson, Young-tae noticed Min-hye was attentive and did her work earnestly. He explained the lessons to her with patience, and encouraged her from time to time. Half way through the session, the domestic helper brought a fresh fruit platter to the study room, which means it was time for a short break.

"Teacher, can I see the silver chain you are wearing?" Min-hye spotted a silver chain on her tutor's neck.

"This silver chain..." Young-tae did not take off his chain, he pulled it out from his shirt and showed it to Min-hye. There was a silver ring hanging on the chain.

"So there is a ring..." Min-hye went closer to take a look, she saw a name engraved on the inner side of the ring.

"Nah Eun-ja...teacher, is Nah Eun-ja your girlfriend?" The name on the ring caught Min-hye's eyes, she thought it must be someone dear to her tutor.

"She was my girlfriend, she passed away in an accident when she was 16." Said Young-tae as he tucked the silver chain and ring under his shirt.

"I'm Sorry to hear that. May I know what happened?" Min-hye was curious as to how the tragedy took place.

"One afternoon, after school, we decided to climb up a tree, the weather was rather windy but it didn't bother us. We went up the tree and sat on one of the branches. Suddenly, a hurricane swept through the area, before we could descend to the ground, we were thrown off balance and fell onto a riverbank, which was lined with stones and pebbles. My head hit the ground and I lost conscious almost instantly. When I regained consciousness, Eun-ja was still lying motionless on the riverbank. She lost a lot of blood from her head and was pronounced dead in the hospital." Young-tae felt pangs of heartache as he recounted the tragedy.

"Oh dear, what a tragedy. You must have gone through a tough time." Min-hye walked to Young-tae and rested her head slightly on his shoulder to express her sympathy.

"She may have passed away, but she will always live in my heart." Min-hye's gesture provided soothing warmth to his heart. He was holding back an urge to embrace her in his arms. At that very moment, he had a strong feeling he could find solace in a cuddle with Min-hye.

"Teacher, how do you usually spend your time during weekends?" Min-hye asked him as she went back to her seat.

"Sometimes I would visit my girlfriend, sometimes I would go painting on an island." Young-tae reorganized his thoughts in response to Min-hye's question.

"I see, would you be going to an island next Saturday? Can I go?" Asked Min-hye, as she thought she deserved a holiday after the tests were over.

"You would feel bored on the island, because I spend most of the time painting. Why not think of some other places, like a theme park, or library, I'll keep you company. Right, you deserve a good break after studying hard for the tests." Said Young-tae.

"I've not gone on an island trip, it sounds like a lot of fun and excitement." Min-hye had been to theme parks several times when she was younger, and going to a library was too boring for her.

"All right, we'll talk about it later, let's get back to the lesson." Agreed Young-tae he would bring her on an island trip, and they carried on with their lesson.

Chp 3

◆

Exhibition for
Amateur Painters

A private art gallery would be showcasing a series of works by local amateur painters for a month. Rui-a was thrilled to have garnered this opportunity for Young-tae. She arranged a meeting for Young-tae to show the manager and the curator of the gallery his paintings. They found his landscape paintings impressive, and encouraged him to have more of his works ready for prospective buyers.

One month before the exhibition, Young-tae spent most of his free time painting in his apartment. He could not afford to spend time travelling to the islands as the exhibition was round the corner.

However, he took a trip to a national park to take some pictures of waterfalls and mountain views, as basis for his paintings. He had asked Min-hye along to replace this excursion with the island trip he promised her earlier on.

"Min-hye, do you want to take a picture in front of the waterfall?" Young-tae was taking pictures of a waterfall.

"Yes, teacher." Min-hye posed in front of the scenery with a big smile as Young-tae took her picture.

"How do you feel about this excursion?" Young-tae asked Min-hye while they were strolling along a mountain trail.

"It's great, I'm feeling energized and refreshed from head to toe." As Min-hye replied Young-tae, she twirled her body slowly in a circle, to show that she truly enjoyed the outdoor activity.

"Hmm...I can see that you're enjoying yourself." Young-tae's face brightened up with a hearty smile when he saw Min-hye's exaggerated body movement.

"Maybe I should become a poet or a painter in future, so that I can be with nature all the time." Min-hye then spread out her hands and twirled her body again in circles.

"Be careful of the uneven ground, don't fall and hurt yourself." Cautioned Young-tae as he moved closer to Min-hye to protect her.

"Teacher, can we go for cakes and ice-creams after lunch?" Min-hye thought of eating dessert after lunch so that she could spend more time with her tutor.

"Sure, but you've to go home after that." Said Young-tae as he needed to get back to his apartment to continue painting for the upcoming exhibition.

"Thank you, teacher." Min-hye was delighted, she was springing and bouncing along the trail, frolicking in nature. Young-tae was fascinated by her youthfulness and innocence charm, he too began to turn himself slowly in circles. The two of them were basking in the misty aura of the rustic mountain.

After taking lunch near the national park, they took the subway back to the city. As agreed in the park, they went to a café for dessert.

"Teacher, can I have that keychain as a gift from you?" As they were eating their cakes in a corner of the café, Min-hye spotted a keychain she fancied at the service counter of the café.

"Which one, the tiny puppy soft toy?" Asked Young-tae as he scoured the range of keychain displayed on the counter.

"Yes, can I have the pink one?" Replied Min-hye, it would be something special if given by her tutor. Young-tae bought it from the counter and gave it to Min-hye.

"Thank you, it's really cute." Min-hye thanked Young-tae with a bright grin, feeling contented that she had earned a keepsake gift from her tutor. In her heart, she was trying to declare her affection for Young-tae.

After dessert, Young-tae accompanied Min-hye back to her house. Min-hye was surprised to see her boyfriend, Seung Ho, waiting outside the mansion. Young-tae bade goodbye to Min-hye as he saw someone was waiting for her.

"Who's that man? Did you go out with him?" Feeling rather uneasy, Seung Ho sized up Young-tae as he walked away from the mansion.

"He's my Maths tutor. We went out for an excursion to a national park." Min-hye told Seung Ho, she then asked him, "Why didn't you tell me you're coming here?"

"I drop by because I miss you. Hmm….are you interested in your tutor?" Seung Ho seemed to be jealous of Young-tae, he was feeling jittery that his girlfriend had gone out with a man.

"Hey, you're over-reacting, it was an excursion just like your teacher take you to a field trip." Min-hye expressed her view to dismiss her boyfriend's worries.

"Promise you won't hang out with him again." Requested Seung Ho, as he sensed something amiss in the atmosphere.

"All right, it's not what you think, don't get jealous for nothing. My parents are not around, want to come into the house?" Min-hye clasped her fingers in his and invited him to her house.

"Yes, let's go in, I'm thirsty." Her tender gesture had lightened up Seung Ho somewhat, he snuggled close to her as they entered the Choi mansion.

The Silver Ring

One evening after work, Young-tae brought a painting to see Dr Kang Woo-hyun. It was a gift for his office where he conducted the therapeutic sessions with his patients.

"Dr Kang, this small painting is for you. Some of my paintings will be showcasing in an exhibition for amateur painters next month, I hope you can attend the cocktail reception on the opening day." The painting Young-tae brought was a picture of colourful Autumn leaves in a mountainous area.

"Thank you, I love this painting, it shows that you've become a professional painter." Praised Dr Kang as he accepted the painting and held it high up against the walls to figure out where he should hang the picture.

"Thank you for the compliment. The cocktail reception will be held in the evening, I'll send you an invitation card next week." Said Young-tae, he had not received the invitation cards from the organizer.

"I should be able to attend the function in the evening, thanks for the invitation. Should we begin the session?" Replied Dr Kang as he placed the painting in a corner of his office.

"Sure." Said Young-tae, without knowing what Dr Kang was going to talk about for the session.

"I noticed you're wearing a silver chain, can I see it?" The silver chain had caught Dr Kang's attention.

Young-tae pulled out the silver chain and ring from his shirt, Dr Kang raised from his chair and leaned forward to take a closer look.

"Hmm…is this the same silver chain you were wearing two or three years back?" Dr Kang recalled that he had seen the silver chain before.

"Yes, I've been wearing it since Eun-ja's death." Said Young-tae, he had told Dr Kang about Eun-ja's death during the previous sessions.

"I wonder how you get this silver ring, fill me in with the details." Dr Kang requested Young-tae to tell him about the ring, while he sat back and relaxed, getting ready for the story.

Young-tae began his story with the days after Eun-ja's funeral.

After Eun-ja's burial ceremony, Young-tae was too distraught to put his mind on his studies. Sometimes he would go to the farm and help out his parents, sometimes he would roam around the suburban area. He would also visit the shaman who performed Eun-ja's funeral ritual, to seek spiritual advice and occasionally help out with her ritual undertakings.

After several months of manual toil in the farm, he saved up a sum of money to buy himself a silver chain and a silver ring. He had the ring engraved with his deceased girlfriend's name 'Nah Eun-ja' and brought it to the shaman to perform a simple rite of solemnization. The shaman placed the silver ring on an altar, as Young-tae kneeled in front of the altar, the shaman began chanting. When she finished chanting, she slid the silver chain and ring down onto Young-tae's neck. When the rite was over, Young-tae handed a token sum of money to the shaman for her service.

"Young-tae, life is full of all sorts of pleasures and miseries, you've to be strong in the face of tough challenges. There'll be sufferings and there'll be joy in your life, remember these are god's will. Prolonged grieving is bad for your life and health, what you need to do is to set a goal and live a fulfilling life. Eun-ja is in heaven now, though you can't see her physical form anymore but she'll live in your heart forever. Let her spirit accompany you as you go through the vicissitudes of life." Moved by Young-tae's conviction, the shaman talked to him and gave him some guidance in life.

"Yes, madam, I'll remember your advice by heart." Replied Young-tae as he listened quietly.

"Did Eun-ja have a dream or goal she would want to pursue in life?" Asked the shaman.

"Yes, she wished to go to the same college with me and upon graduation, she would look for a job in a bank." Young-tae recalled the plan Eun-ja had when she was alive.

"I see, do you think it's important to turn her wishes into reality? Would you feel better if you could fulfil her dream?" Inquired the shaman.

"Yes, madam, her dream is as important as mine, and I definitely will feel better if I can fulfil her dream." Replied Young-tae as he imagined Eun-ja would be happy if he could do that.

"Then you should go back to school and start pursuing your goal." Advised the shaman.

"Yes, madam, I'll resume schooling next year." Young-tae accepted her advice, he bowed slightly to the shaman to express his gratitude. From then on, Young-tae had only one goal in life, which was to make Eun-ja's dream come true.

"I see. Let's take a break, I'll be back in a minute." Said Dr Kang as he stood up and went out of the office. He came back holding two cups of tea, one for himself and one for Young-tae.

"Hmm…I can see this ring means a lot to you, I would say its importance is equivalent to your own life, am I right to say that?" After listening to Young-tae's recollection, Dr Kang expressed his opinion as he took a sip of his tea.

"Maybe that's true, the ring is important to me. Thanks for the tea." Replied Young-tae, as he lifted the cup and took a sip of the tea.

"It's amazing that because of this ring, you were able to calm down and concentrate on your studies, and stick to the goal of fulfilling Eun-ja's dream. You went to college and now you're working in a bank. Which means this ring helps you achieve your success today, without it, you might still be toiling in the farm?" Commented Dr Kang, as he looked at Young-tae, expecting a response from him.

"Well, since I've been wearing this ring after Eun-ja passed away, I can't imagine the situation in which I'm not wearing this ring. However, your assumption might be accurate. Then again, if not for this ring, I might have something else as reminiscent of Eun-ja." Replied Young-tae as he took another sip of tea, and carried on with the discussion.

"I was full of guilt when I face her parents, no amount of condolences could assuage the grief of losing their daughter. At that time, I thought, I would do anything for them, when they requested a marriage ritual, I fully agreed and it was carried out the next day when Eun-ja's body was sent back home." Young-tae explained his decision for the marriage ritual with Eun-ja.

"I remember you told me about the marriage ritual between you and Eun-ja's body." Said Dr Kang, he sat back and encouraged Young-tae to continue with his recollection.

"My mental psyche had totally collapsed, all day long I couldn't think of anything else but to blame myself for her death. The advice from the shaman was like a light at the other end of the tunnel, my spirit was lifted as I found a meaning in my life. I resumed schooling the next year, and was determined in pursuing Eun-ja's dream." Young-tae gave credit to the shaman who gave him the advice.

"Right, you've been doing well since then." Agreed Dr Kang, then he continued, "I'm curious, have you ever separated from your ring before? I mean, you've been wearing it for two decades, surely there would be times you need to take it off?"

"No, not really. The hook of the old silver chain was damaged, I have to get a new one. The chain I'm wearing is new, but the silver ring is the original one." Recalled Young-tae when the old silver chain came loose one day when he was changing into a shirt in his apartment.

"I see, would you feel the same if you keep your ring in a jewellery box at home? I mean, you still have the ring but you're not wearing it." Said Dr Kang hypothetically.

"Hmm…I've not tried putting it in a box and leave it at home. I mean, wearing it makes me feel calm and secured, I need to have Eun-ja close to me." Young-tae was rather forthcoming with his feelings.

"Enough about the silver ring. Let's say you become bored with working in the bank, what kind of job would you prefer to do?" Dr Kang switched to another subject as he knew it would be quite impossible to get Young-tae to part with his ring.

"Hmm..I've not given much thought about that. Basically it's a stable job and I've gained valuable experience after working in the industry since I graduated. I might switch to work in another bank but I'll not leave the industry." Replied Young-tae as he was quite sure he would work in a bank until he retired.

"So you'll never be bored of working in the bank?" Asked Dr Kang again, perhaps he was trying to find out the true reason behind Young-tae's decision to stay in the industry, that is to fulfil Eun-ja's dream.

"Not really, it's quite challenging to work in a bank, the banking products and services we sell benefit everybody in the society, we take pride in that." Explained Young-tae further.

"So you are not staying in the job because of Eun-ja?" Dr Kang continued with his questioning.

"Well, whether I do this for Eun-ja or not is beside the issue now. I don't have other work experience except the banking experience, so it's not easy for me to switch industry. Even if I stay in the job solely for Eun-ja's sake, it's not really a bad thing, don't you agree?" Young-tae was determined to stay in the industry.

"Well then, you are right to say that. Let's call it a day. I'll see you again soon." Dr Kang declared the session over.

"Thank you. I'll send the invitation card to you next week. See you at the cocktail reception." Young-tae reminded Dr Kang of the cocktail reception for his exhibition before he left his office.

Cocktail Reception

The cocktail reception was held on a Friday evening, VIPs and guests were invited to grace the opening day of the exhibition. It was supposed to be a delightful and relax function where the guests were not obliged to purchase paintings. The gallery was filled with classical music and chatting noises. Guests were seen mingling in the crowd, some of them held a glass of champagne while chatting away, others were just drinking orange juices or plain water.

Young-tae was discussing the paintings on the walls with other artists, they exchanged opinions and moved from one area to another. Occasionally, the manager of the gallery would introduce Young-tae to guests who showed interest in his paintings. After he left the other artists, Young-tae positioned himself near his paintings to entertain interested guests.

Rui-a was chatting with a gentleman when she saw Dr Kang walked into the gallery. She excused herself from the guest and took a glass of champagne for Dr Kang.

"Dr Kang, thanks for coming to the exhibition." Rui-a shook hands with Dr Kang and passed him the glass of champagne.

"Good evening Rui-a, nice to see you again." Greeted Dr Kang as he received the champagne.

"Let's go look for Young-tae, he's somewhere near his paintings." Said Rui-a as she accompanied Dr Kang to the exhibition hall.

"Rui-a, that gentleman was looking at you, do you know him well?" Dr Kang noticed there was a guest kept looking at Rui-a.

"I was chatting with him before you came, he's just an acquaintance." Rui-a looked to the direction of the young man mentioned by Dr Kang, she saw the gentleman was smiling at her, she nodded her head politely in return.

"Hi, Dr Kang, thanks for coming." A good spirited Young-tae shook hands with Dr Kang.

"Congratulations on your first exhibition! The paintings show off your mastery skills, the way you mixed the colours, and the rugged texture of your paintings, really compliment the nature of the landscapes. They are truly impressive works." Commended Dr Kang as he admired Young-tae's artistic achievement.

"Thanks for the flattering remark, I've more faith in my paintings now." Dr Kang's praises gave an instant boost to Young-tae's confidence.

"Rui-a, that gentleman has his gaze fixed on you, I think he is attracted to you." Observed Dr Kang as he noticed the love struck man could not take his eyes off Rui-a while talking to his friends. Young-tae turned his head out of curiosity in search of the gentleman, and he saw a well-dressed, good looking young man stealing glances at Rui-a.

"Well, I've to thank Rui-a for securing the opportunity for my paintings to be exhibited here, she's such a dear." In the face of a potential suitor, Young-tae promptly displayed his affectionate relationship with Rui-a. He held her hand close to his chest and looked at her with a warm and endearing smile. Instinctively, Rui-a huddled near Young-tae, looking at him with a loving gaze.

Dampened by the intimacy between Rui-a and her boyfriend, the young man turned his head at once to the other direction. He then bade goodbye to his friends and left the gallery.

"Oh, he's heartbroken, he's leaving the gallery." Dr Kang lowered his voice discreetly, as he saw the young man walked out of the gallery. Young-tae and Rui-a turned their heads and saw the young man headed towards the lift lobby.

"Ahh…I thought he was a potential buyer, hopefully he would return soon to pick up some of the paintings exhibited here. He was rather enthusiastic when he talked about the paintings earlier on." Said Rui-a, slightly disappointed with the outcome.

"He showed enthusiasm in the paintings because he was attracted to you, simple as that. Hmm….I see you're getting more attractive each day, Young-tae, don't you agree?" Dr Kang thought Rui-a was a confident and charming beauty, perhaps Young-tae should be mindful of potential suitors.

"I know you're afraid someone might snatch her away from me, right? I know you mean well." Young-tae was aware of Dr Kang's concern over his personal affair, he patted Dr Kang's shoulder to show his appreciation.

"I'll make a move now, thanks for inviting me to the function. I'll come by to look at the paintings again when I'm free." Said Dr Kang as he bade goodbye to both of them.

"The exhibition will be on for a month, you can drop by during lunch time as well. Thanks for coming." Rui-a truly hoped that Dr Kang would return and purchase some of the paintings.

"Thanks for coming, Dr Kang, I'll see you soon." Said Young-tae, and they accompanied Dr Kang to the lift lobby.

At the end of the cocktail reception, several paintings were sold, Young-tae's painting was one of them. The manager told him to get ready other paintings should the sold paintings were to be taken down and delivered to the customers.

Both Young-tae and Rui-a were thrilled that he had one painting sold on the opening day. They were exhilarated by the encouraging news when they left the gallery.

"Are you hungry? Should we go for supper?" Young-tae asked Rui-a when they got into his car.

"Yes, I'm a little hungry, what do you feel like eating?" Rui-a's stomach was quite empty after walking around the gallery entertaining guests for a couple of hours.

"A bowl of piping hot stew is just what I need in this cold breezy night." Said Young-tae in a heightened mood.

"Sounds good, I'll have chicken stew with kimchi." Replied Rui-a in a cheery tone.

They stopped by a korean restaurant for supper before they headed home.

"Rui-a, I'm really grateful for the work you've done for me, thank you my dear." Gazing her eyes with affection, Young-tae put his hand on Rui-a's to show his gratitude.

"It's really a pleasure to see your paintings are well received by the public, I'm truly thrilled. I'm so proud of you." Rui-a looked into his eyes with a sense of pride. It was a wonderful night, the mood in the air was sublime for the lovey-dovey couple.

"We've been together for ten years, I think it's about time we tie the knot, what do you think?" Asked Young-tae, perhaps the love struck young man who fancied Rui-a at the cocktail reception was the impetus to his proposal.

"I see you're jealous because a good looking guy fancies me at the gallery, right?" Rui-a did not say yes to his proposal, she was not satisfied that Young-tae popped the question because he was threatened by a potential suitor.

"All right, you guessed it, it never crossed my mind that you might leave me for another guy until I see it with my own eyes today. I'm sorry, I take things for granted for too long." Apologized Young-tae, feeling guilty he had taken their relationship for granted in the past years.

"Do you want to marry me solely because you love me? You shouldn't marry me out of convenience, I mean, it might be that you can't find the perfect partner in the past years, so you give up looking and decide to marry me." Rui-a was trying to get Young-tae to tell her his true feelings towards her, as she thought they should not take the holy matrimony lightly.

"I'm not sensitive enough towards your feelings, it's my fault. I love you, that's the only reason I want to marry you. Would you marry me?" Proposed Young-tae again, anticipating earnestly for Rui-a's consent.

"Yes." Rui-a accepted his marriage proposal, although she did not doubt his love for her, she needed to hear the right reason for his proposal.

"Should we hold the wedding ceremony next year?" A happy Young-tae suggested a time for the wedding.

"Spring should be a good time for a wedding." Rui-a was overjoyed that Young-tae had finally set a time for their marriage. She was almost in tears with the sudden proposal, as up till then, she had no idea if Young-tae had loved her enough to marry her, even though they had been a couple for a decade.

"All right then, we'll have a Spring wedding next year." Agreed with Rui-a for a Spring wedding, Young-tae patted her hand gently as a gesture to confirm his decision. During supper, they talked about the exhibition and his paintings, and decided to visit the gallery over the weekends until the exhibition was over.

Chp 4

◆

Toast for a Brighter Future

The exhibition for the amateur painters went on smoothly. By the second week, a handful of paintings were sold. Most of the paintings were bought by avid art collectors who commented that the amateur painters' works were inspiring and invigorating. Occasionally, Young-tae would drop by the gallery to discuss the sale of his paintings and the exhibition with the manager. Sometimes Rui-a would join him for dinner with the gallery manager.

One evening, Rui-a came out of a client's office after a meeting. As the office was a few blocks away from the gallery, she decided to visit the exhibition before going home. With her laptop bag slung over her shoulder and a handbag held in one hand, she exited the client's office building via the main entrance.

"Miss Rui-a!" The gentleman whom Rui-a talked to at the opening day of the exhibition was walking pass by the building that evening. He called out her name at the building entrance. Rui-a looked at him in a state of stupor before she recognized him as her 'potential suitor' from the gallery.

"Good evening, it's you, what a coincidence." It took Rui-a a few seconds to utter her greetings as she was surprise to see the gentleman.

"Good evening, it's nice to see you again. Do you work here?" The young man was delighted to meet Rui-a, his love interest, in a chance meeting.

"I don't work here, I'm here for a meeting with a client. I'm sorry I did not catch your name the other day." Replied Rui-a, feeling rather embarrassed as she could not remember his name.

"Here, this is my name card, I'm Seung Jae." The young man introduced himself and passed her a name card.

"Do you work in this area?" Holding the name card, Rui-a was surprised he was a general manager of a real estate company, as he looked rather young for a general manager. Out of courtesy, she exchanged her name card with him. Seung Jae took a glance at her name card and kept it in his pocket.

"So you're an architect, hmm...I suppose you're a busy person." Commented Seung Jae. Then he replied, "My office is just next to this building. It must be a lucky day for me to bump into you under such circumstances, should we go for a cup of coffee?" Although not as 'love struck' as before, Seung Jae apparently had a romantic interest in her, so he tried his luck to have a little rendezvous with her.

"I'm sorry, I don't drink coffee in the evening. I'll make a move now." Rui-a turned down his suggestion politely, and indicated that she was leaving.

"That's fine. Would you be going to the gallery? I would like to visit it again, some of the paintings seem to be quite suitable to display in my office." Seung Jae thought visiting the exhibition would stand a better chance for him to spend some time with Rui-a.

"Are you free to visit the gallery now? Actually I'm going there right now." Since Seung Jae had shown interest in the paintings, Rui-a was willing to accompany him to the gallery, it would be unwise to let pass a potential customer.

"That's great, let's go now. Come, let me carry the laptop for you." Seung Jae took over her laptop bag to lighten her load.

"Thank you. Do you visit the gallery often?" Rui-a was rather impressed by his gentlemanly behaviour.

"About once a month. This exhibition is rather interesting, the abstract paintings are intriguing. I don't have a preference yet, but you know, if I could relate to the message the artist was trying to express in his work, I might buy one of those paintings." Explained Seung Jae, he was thinking whether Rui-a's boyfriend was the abstract artist.

"Would your boyfriend be at the gallery this evening?" Asked Seung Jae, hoping Young-tae would not be there so as to avoid any awkwardness. The scene in which Young-tae and Rui-a displayed their affection at the opening day of the exhibition was still vivid in his mind.

"He won't be there today, he's busy." Young-tae was giving tuition that evening, though Rui-a did not feel the need to tell her acquaintance the detail.

"Is your boyfriend the abstract painter?" Seung Jae was relieved Young-tae would not be at the gallery that evening.

"He's the landscape painter, his name is Joo Young-tae." Replied Rui-a, she thought of introducing Young-tae and his works to Seung Jae in more details later.

"I see, landscape paintings can be rather popular and sellable, is that right?" Perhaps Seung Jae might purchase some of his paintings to please Rui-a.

"Quite true, some customers enquired about his paintings in the past few days." Concurred Rui-a.

They arrived at the gallery, feeling they had known each other a little bit better. While touring the exhibition hall, they exchanged opinions about the art works. At the end of the tour, Seung Jae bought a landscape painting and an abstract painting without much hesitation. He paid for them and requested for them to be delivered to his office. Indeed, Rui-a was pleased with his purchases, it seemed to her that Seung Jae's penchant for paintings was genuine.

"Thank you so much, Mr Seung Jae. I think I should treat you to dinner, to show my appreciation for purchasing the paintings." Rui-a was happy to play host for a dinner to her customer.

"How can I resist a dinner treat from you? Let's go." Though Seung Jae knew she was doing it for her boyfriend, he was still thrilled and readily accepted the invitation.

The exhibition came to an end one month later. Young-tae had seven of his paintings sold. To him, his debut exhibition had achieved extraordinary success. As for Rui-a, the person who earned the opportunity to showcase his paintings, she was immensely pleased with the outcome, and was glad that the effort she put in was worthwhile.

On the last day of the exhibition, they bought a bottle of champagne and some delicacies from a shopping mall before they headed home for a mini celebration with Mdm Shim and Joo-a. Just before dinner, champagne glasses were filled and delicacies laid out on the dining table. Rui-a, Young-tae, Mdm Shim and Joo-a gathered around the dining table to celebrate the success of Young-tae's debut exhibition.

"Let me propose a toast, it's for Young-tae to become a successful painter in future." Said Rui-a as she raised her glass of champagne in the air. Young-tae and Mdm Shim raised their champagne as well, Joo-a was holding a cup of soft drink.

"I toast for a brighter future for Young-tae and Rui-a." Mdm Shim followed with a toast.

"I hope brother would become wealthy." Joo-a proposed a straightforward toast, her rather wacky toast brought a smile to everybody's face.

"I toast for all to live a happy and peaceful life." Finally Young-tae gave his toast. They congregated their glasses and cup in mid-air, and tapped slightly to meet all glasses and cup before they put down their hands and sipped on their own beverage.

"Mom, I'll be moving to Young-tae's apartment after the wedding, is that all right?" Rui-a told Mdm Shim about her plan.

"There are more rooms in this house, why not sell Young-tae's apartment and live with us?" Mdm Shim spoke matter-of-factly, with the hope that they could live under the same roof with the newly-weds.

"I mean we need to have some privacy, for a period of time, maybe half a year or one year. We'll need your help if I become pregnant, then we'll move back here, or buy a new house, is that all right?" Explained Rui-a, as agreed previously between Young-tae and herself.

"All right, make sure you two don't fight when I'm not around." Said Mdm Shim reluctantly.

"Auntie, don't worry, I won't fight with Rui-a. When we've a child we'll move in with you and Joo-a." Assured Young-tae with a promise to Mdm Shim.

"I understand, you two need privacy after you get married. Anyway, I'm so happy for the two of you, I'm going back to our hometown next week to tell Rui-a's father about the wedding, he would be so pleased to hear the news." To Mdm Shim, she had no doubt that Young-tae would be his son-in-law eventually, and he would be a devoted, dutiful and loyal husband to her daughter.

"Mom, we need to shop for a pair of wedding bands tomorrow, let's go shopping and take dinner at a restaurant, are you all right with it?" Rui-a suggested a shopping trip and a family dinner.

"That's great, let's all go out for dinner tomorrow. There are so many things to prepare for a wedding, have you decided the venue to hold the wedding?" The good-natured Mdm Shim was upbeat about her daughter's wedding, contemplating what she could do on her big day.

"We're thinking of holding an outdoor ceremony in the afternoon. Since we only have a few months to prepare, we'll keep it as simple as possible. Moreover, we don't have a big budget for the wedding." Young-tae thought Rui-a had a busy work schedule, it would not be practical to spend too much time on preparing the wedding.

A Vicious Attack

The exhibition ended a month later. Young-tae decided to spend a day on Ganghwa island even though the weather was cold at the end of the year. On a Saturday morning, he woke up early to get ready for his island trip. He cooked a bowl of ramen for breakfast. Since he woke up, he was absorbed in the events of his debut exhibition. After breakfast, he packed his painting equipment steadfastly and set off his journey in good spirit.

It takes ninety minutes to travel from Seoul to Ganghwa Island. There is a bridge connecting the island and the mainland. As soon as he arrived on the island, Young-tae took a bus to bring him near the foot of the mountain. He intended to hike along the mountain trail and set up his easel on a spot where he could take in the panoramic view of the island's rice fields and surrounding islands. After the bus ride, he walked along the road to the entrance of the mountain trail. A young lady on a bike rode passed him on the opposite side of the road.

"Brother Young-tae!" A young, sprightly lady on the bike waved and called out for Young-tae with a wide smile from across the road.

"Hey, Suk-mi! See you later." Young-tae turned his head to the young lady, Suk-mi, waved and greeted her in return. Suk-mi kept on cycling in the opposite direction and gradually faded away in his vision.

It was a refreshing walk in the cool morning breeze, Young-tae strolled leisurely to the foot of the mountain and climbed up the mountain trail made up of big chunks of rock slabs. The forest scent in the mountain was so fresh that Young-tae thought it was worthwhile to visit this island just for the crisp and rustic mountain air. He inhaled and exhaled with deep breaths while ascending the trail, as though to cleanse and purify the air in his lungs.

As he came to the peak of the mountain, Young-tae set up his easel on a patch of even ground. The bird's eye view from the mountain was spectacular. Flying unflaggingly with their wings wide spread, a flock of white seagulls whirled above the sea water in a wavelike manner. The birds complement the sea view and made it a perfect picture for his painting.

When he was done with the photo taking, he started sketching the outline of the picture on the canvas. Too engrossed with his work, he was not aware a man was sneaking up on him from behind.

"Thwack!" All of a sudden, Young-tae's back and neck was bludgeoned by the stranger with a block of wood, his body bent forward as he felt a sharp pain in the back of his neck. Not giving him a chance to retaliate, the man bludgeoned him again. Young-tae's back was struck again and he fell prostrate on the ground. He tried to turn his body around to the assailant, but before he could do that, he was bludgeoned again by the attacker.

"Scumbag, don't ever let me see you again!" The attacker shouted at Young-tae, but Young-tae could not defend himself as he had fell and was groaning in great pain on the ground. In his faint consciousness, it seemed to him that the attacker knew him. At this juncture, Suk-mi, the young lady Young-tae greeted earlier in the morning, came to the mountain and witnessed the attack.

"Stop it! I'm calling the police! Stop it!" Cried Suk-mi as she saw the assailant was about to strike Young-tae again. The man threw the block of wood and scampered down the mountain trail when he saw Suk-mi, who threatened to call the police.

"Brother Young-tae, are you all right?" Suk-mi hurried over to look at Young-tae's injuries. She started to feel nervous as there was a trickle of blood coming out of his mouth.

"Suk-mi....do you...know the...attacker?" Trying to string his words together while suffering tremendous pain on his neck and back, Young-tae asked Suk-mi whether she recognized the assailant as he thought that the attacker seemed to know him.

"I'm sorry, he's my boyfriend. I asked for a breakup a few weeks ago, he didn't want to break up with me. So I told him about having an intimate affair with you to make him leave me, and he finally agreed. Little did I know he would take revenge by assaulting you." It was unexpected to Suk-mi that her boyfriend would become violent and take it out on Young-tae over their breakup.

"I see...Don't...blame...yourself...can you help.... to pack...the painting stuff....into my bags?" Requested Young-tae as he struggled to maintain his consciousness.

"Yes.." Replied Suk-mi, then she swiftly collected his painting equipment and then packed them into his haversack. She then folded the easel and drawing board and put them into his large canvas bag.

"Suk-mi...I can't...move my body...use the... handphone...to call an...ambulance...119..." After he knew it was Suk-mi's boyfriend who attacked him, he told Suk-mi to call the ambulance. Suk-mi searched for the mobile phone in his bag and called 119.

"If the police investigates…tell them…it's a robbery… tell them you…don't know…the attacker…" Cautioned Young-tae, as their affairs would be exposed if her boyfriend was arrested.

"All right…I understand…" Replied Suk-mi after she made the emergency call.

"Suk-mi…I came here today….to tell you…that I'll be…getting married…next Spring…" Young-tae told Suk-mi about his impending wedding, it was like telling a good friend a piece of good news.

"I see, congratulations…take a rest, the ambulance will be here soon." Said a disappointed Suk-mi, though she did not dream of maintaining a lasting relationship with Young-tae, she was nonetheless saddened by the news.

The staff from the ambulance had to carry Young-tae in a stretcher when descending the mountain trail. It was hard work for the staff as they needed to synchronize their steps and balance the stretcher, so as not to cause too much motion to the patient who was suffering from neck and back injuries.

Suk-mi helped to carry his bags to the ambulance and accompanied him to the local hospital.

At the hospital, a doctor examined his neck and back injuries, and sent him for an X-ray. He was put on a neck brace as there was a minor fracture on his neck, as well as muscle and ligament tear. Fortunately, his injuries were not serious enough to undergo a surgery. A course of antibiotics and pain-killer pills were prescribed by the doctor. However, he needed to stay in the hospital for a few days for his condition to stabilize before he could be discharged.

"Suk-mi, can you take out the battery charger from the side pocket of my haversack and charge my handphone?" Suk-mi was sitting by Young-tae's bedside in a ward.

"Are you going to call your girlfriend?" Asked Suk-mi while she took the charger, plug it into the power point and connect it to the hand-phone.

"Not today, she's busy, I think she'll call me tomorrow." Said Young-tae. "I'm hungry, can you buy some snacks for me? Get the money from my wallet."

"My mom boiled some ginseng chicken soup this afternoon, I'll get some for you." Suk-mi suggested a home cooked nutritious soup instead.

"Sounds good, but ask for your mom's permission first." Young-tae smiled at Suk-mi to show his appreciation.

Half an hour later Suk-mi returned with the ginseng chicken soup, rice, pickled vegetables and a set of Korean traditional playing cards. After dinner, Suk-mi moved a small table to Young-tae's bedside for their card game.

"Last month, some of my paintings were sold in an exhibition. You know, all the time I've spent on paintings and on the trips to the islands are worthwhile." Young-tae told Suk-mi about his debut exhibition.

"Really! That's cool! You're going to be famous!" Exclaimed Suk-mi, her cheery smile was contagious.

"Hmm…being famous can be stressful though..ha.. ha.." Young-tae's head movement was limited by the neck brace, he could only laugh softly with the stiff neck.

"Suk-mi, I'd like to buy you a gift for calling the ambulance and taking me to the hospital, I must repay your kindness." Young-tae made a suggestion to show his gratitude.

"Don't worry about the trivial, you got injured because of me, how can I receive a gift from you?" Suk-mi felt sorry that her boyfriend attacked and injured Young-tae, she should not receive any gift from him.

"Maybe you've an inspiration you wish to achieve in life, such as, to become a fashion designer, or a hair stylist, ahh...I remember you told me you want to be a bakery chef, if you're still interested, I'll pay the course fees, what do you think?" Young-tae recalled she had told him about her interest in baking cakes and pastries.

"Yes, I dream of becoming a bakery chef one day, but I can't just take your money. I mean, you're not my father or brother, it's awkward." Suk-mi rejected his suggestion outright.

"It won't cost a lot of money, take it as a sponsorship from a friend. Suk-mi, after today's incident, I might not be visiting this island anymore, though I don't bear a grudge against your boyfriend, but I find it better for me to stay away, at least for a period of time. Moreover, I'll be getting married soon, this might be the last time we see each other." The atmosphere became sombre when Young-tae spoke in a rather serious tone.

"Sorry, it's my fault that you're being attacked." Suk-mi was saddened by the eventuality of the day's incident, she began to sob silently, "Brother Young-tae, I'll miss you dearly." Declared Suk-mi of her affection for Young-tae, thinking it might well be the last time they see each other.

"Silly girl, stop crying. That's why I said you need to take up a course, if you take the course in Seoul, then we can see each other more often." Explained Young-tae, half teasing Suk-mi.

"Really...but you're getting married, it's not convenient to meet up with me anymore." Suk-mi was not sure whether they should continue their friendship after Young-tae got married.

"It's all right to have female friends for me after I got married, don't worry about it. It would be great if you become a successful bakery chef in future." Young-tae persuaded her to pursue her dream in life.

"All right, thank you, brother Young-tae." Nodded Suk-mi to express her gratitude. Gone was the sadness on her face, which was replaced with a cheerful demeanour as her mind was filled with hope, she was about to begin a journey to pursue her aspiration.

"I'll find a suitable course for you when I return to Seoul, wait for my news." Young-tae patted Suk-mi's hand to assure her that he would keep his promise.

Perhaps Young-tae was feeling guilty for having an intimate affair with Suk-mi, thus prompted him to atone for his impulsive acts, to realize her dream should redeem his guilt somewhat. Since he had earned some money from his paintings, he would be able to pay the course fees for her. Or perhaps, Suk-mi's dream was like Eun-ja's dream, it was a sacred duty for him to make her dream come true.

Suk-mi returned to the hospital the next morning to play cards with Young-tae again. In the afternoon, Young-tae's phone rang.

"Are you at home? Why didn't you call me yesterday?" After lunch, Rui-a called up Young-tae, she had returned from the local market in the neighbourhood with her mother and sister.

"I'm still at Ganghwado, I met with an accident yesterday, I'm hospitalised." Replied Young-tae without much strength, apparently he was tortured by the pain on his stiff neck and sore back.

"What?! Are your seriously injured? Why didn't you call earlier?" Rui-a was getting anxious and raised her voice slightly. She was edgy because he did not inform her on the very day of his hospitalisation.

"My neck and back are injured, I'm wearing a neck brace, don't worry, it's not really serious." Hearing the resentment and worry in her voice, Young-tae described his injuries in a casual manner so as to ease the tension.

"I'm going over right now." His injuries and the belated news was equally unsettling to Rui-a, but all she could do was to go to the hospital as soon as possible.

"All right, take my car, and remember to fill up some petrol." Reminded Young-tae in a relaxed tone.

In the late afternoon, Rui-a, Mdm Shim and Joo-a arrived at the hospital. Young-tae gave a brief account of his encounter with a 'robber' to the trio: he was attacked from behind by a stranger welding a block of wood in his hand, but the robber did not manage to rob him off any valuables because someone came to the mountain just in time. He was saved by a local who called the ambulance and sent him to the hospital.

"I'm so worried, why didn't you tell me about this yesterday?" Rui-a's voice was almost trembling, looking at his injuries, she was closed to tears. Sitting next to Rui-a was Mdm Shim, she looked tensed and worried as well.

"I'm sorry, I was really exhausted yesterday, I needed a good rest." Explained Young-tae, hopefully this reason could appease her anxiety.

"I understand, but you should at least give me a call." Rui-a insisted he should inform her on the day of his hospitalisation.

"What's the point, you would be worried sick at home, or probably rushed over here. Brother said he needed to rest yesterday." Joo-a joined in their conversation and obviously supported Young-tae's decision.

"Don't dwell on the trivial, go and check with the doctor whether I can be discharged today." Young-tae gave her an errand to distract her attention from the subject.

So Rui-a went to see the doctor and requested for Young-tae to be discharged so that she could bring him home on that Sunday, her reason being it would be inconvenient for her to come to the hospital again on a weekday.

The care and concern of the trio had touched Young-tae's heartstrings on this cold Sunday evening. They brought warmth to his heart when they visited the hospital, though they were not related by blood, he was blessed to be able to relish the greatness and sweetness of their kinship. As for himself, he should love and cherish them wholeheartedly in return.

Chp 5

◆

Bakery Course for Suk-mi

Young-tae's unfortunate encounter on the island had temporary disrupted his life, he applied for a month's leave and stayed at home to recuperate. During his recovery, he was accompanied by Mdm Shim and Joo-a in the day, and Rui-a would visit him after work. The three of them would then return to their home when Young-tae went to bed.

Young-tae was still plagued by his injuries during the first week, his neck was stiff and his back was sore. However, under Mdm Shim's care, he was served with three nutritious meals a day, thus, his condition improved speedily into the second week of his recuperation. He began to surf the internet for a bakery course for Suk-mi.

"Auntie, thank you for taking care of me in the past weeks, since I'm getting better now, maybe you should take some rest at home, you don't have to take care of me starting next week." Young-tae made an excuse hoping for Mdm Shim and Joo-a to stop visiting him so that he could bring Suk-mi to the bakery training school to register for a course.

"I'm not tired at all, don't worry, I'll stay here until you're fully recovered." Mdm Shim patted Young-tae's arm as she was glad Young-tae had acknowledged her dedication in taking care of him. She had agreed with Rui-a that she would help out at his apartment until his neck brace was removed.

During the third week, Young-tae was looking for an excuse to go out and fetch Suk-mi to Seoul, he told Mdm Shim he needed to pick up some toiletries from the shopping mall, however, Mdm Shim insisted to tag along as she needed to buy some grocery from the supermarket as well. Young-tae had no choice but to postpone his meeting with Suk-mi.

Later on that day, Young-tae came up with another excuse, he told Rui-a he needed the car to send his laptop for repair, and that Mdm Shim and Joo-a did not have to accompany him.

The next morning, Young-tae drove all the way to Ganghwa Island to fetch Suk-mi to the culinary training school. While she was there, she studied the brochures and was interested in a beginner's course. Young-tae filled up an enrolment form and paid for a three-month course, after which, they went to a fast food restaurant in a shopping mall for lunch.

"Suk-mi, are you feeling anxious about taking a course in Seoul?" Young-tae asked Suk-mi as she had never studied or lived in Seoul before, life in Seoul would be different from that of the island.

"I really enjoy coming here, it's so different from the island, there're so many buildings and so many shops. Brother Young-tae, thank you, you're the most generous person I've ever met." Seoul was like a kaleidoscope to Suk-mi, there are many interesting things to see and do here. It was an eye-opener for the sprightly young lady.

"I'm glad you are comfortable here, don't keep quiet if someone trample on you, I mean, if you encounter any problem, let me know." Young-tae was concerned about her adaptability to the new environment.

"Don't worry, I know how to take care of myself." Replied Suk-mi with a bright smile, her face exuded plenty of self-confidence.

"What about renting a place in Seoul when the course starts? It would be time consuming and tiring for you to travel back and forth between Seoul and Ganghwado." Young-tae thought maybe he should look for a place for her in Seoul.

"I'll take public transport for the time being since I can't afford to rent a place here. Moreover, I need to help look after my younger brother and do some chores at home." Other than a budget constraint, Suk-mi explained that she also had duties at home.

"I see…I suppose you can't ignore your duties at home." Young-tae suddenly became silent as an idea crossed his mind.

"Upon completing my course, I'd look for a job, then I probably would need to rent a place here." While Suk-mi envisaged a work life in Seoul after she completed the course, she noticed the sudden change of mood in Young-tae, she waited for him to pick up the conversation again.

"I was thinking if you're comfortable you can stay in my apartment, you don't have to pay me rental. My apartment is small, I'll clear the stuff in the study room and put a bed there." Young-tae was acting in good faith, hopefully, the arrangement could make Suk-mi live and study comfortably in Seoul.

"Thank you, but you're getting married soon, I shouldn't cause any inconvenience to you." Suk-mi was tempted by the offer, but she turned him down. "Moreover, your wife-to-be will not be pleased if I live under the same roof with you."

"Suk-mi, you know I suggested this without any ulterior motive, I mean to help you as much as I could." Young-tae assured her of his well intention.

"I understand you mean well." Suk-mi had his marriage in mind, she was grateful that Young-tae had sponsored the bakery course, and it would be wrong for her to create problem for his marriage.

"All right, let's go to the book shop and get some bakery books." Suk-mi's sensible and calm presence had attracted Young-tae since the first day he met her, he was glad that she had grown to be more mature and independent. They left the fast food restaurant and went to City's Bookshop, which was on the second floor of the shopping mall.

Seung Brothers

Seung Jae was sitting at the café next to City's Bookshop sipping a cup of tea. Through the glass panels of the café, he saw a man wearing a neck brace passed by the café. He thought that man looked familiar to him. He then saw him threw a leaflet or a brochure into a rubbish bin outside the café. Next to the man was a young lady with long straight hair. While trying to recall who that person was, Seung Jae's phone rang.

"Jae, where are you? I've just entered the shopping mall." Seung Ho was meeting his eldest brother, Seung Jae, for a shopping trip.

"I'm at the café next to City's Bookshop, come up here." Replied Seung Jae. Seung Ho was his youngest brother, they met to shop for presents for Seung Jae's second younger brother, Seung Hyuk's birthday.

"Okay, see you there." Seung Ho hung up his phone and took the escalator up to the café. He passed by the book shop and a man wearing a neck brace caught his attention, which he thought he had seen that man before. Before he could figure out who that person was, he arrived at the café, spotted his brother and went over and sat opposite him.

"Ho, what would you like to eat or drink?" Seung Jae asked his brother when he sat down.

"Nothing for me, I had lunch at home. Have you bought a present for Hyuk?" Asked Seung Ho.

"Not yet, I'm taking a break here after meeting a client. Let's go to the men's department after I finish my tea." Seung Jae took a sip of his tea and looked outside of the café, hoping to get a glimpse of that person with the neck brace again.

"You saw someone you know?" Asked Seung Ho, as Seung Jae was casting his vision outside the café.

"There's this person wearing a neck brace, I thought I saw him somewhere before..." Seung Jae said to his brother, as he tried hard to recall who the familiar face was.

"I saw that person at the book shop. He looked familiar to me too." Seung Ho thought that person looked like Min-hye's Mathematics tutor.

"Really, who is he…right…he's a painter, I bought his painting from an exhibition not long ago." Seung Jae finally recognized that man was Young-tae, the painter. The painting on the wall of the café gave him the connection between Young-tae and paintings.

"I thought he looked like Min-hye's tuition teacher." Seung Ho told his brother his discovery.

"You met Min-hye's tutor before?" Asked Seung Jae curiously, "Are we talking about the same person?"

"I met him once outside Min-hye's house. She went out with him to a national park as a reward for her good test results." Seung Ho recalled he saw Young-tae while waiting for Min-hye at the front gate of the Choi mansion.

"A dedicated tutor I suppose." Seung Jae's own observation and Seung Ho's story befuddled him somewhat, then he asked, "But that guy looked like the painter I know, do you know the young lady next to him?"

"I didn't see her face clearly, it's too far away. Could she be his sister or cousin or another student? It would be peculiar if they are friends, considering their wide age gap." Seung Ho made a fair presumption.

"Right, she might well be his sister. What if they are friends?" Seung Jae did not feel good to suggest something improper or unethical, but the seemingly unusual occurrence was mind-boggling to him.

As they raised their queries, Young-tae and Suk-mi exited the bookshop.

"They came out of the book shop, don't look out of the café." Seung Jae sighted the duo and reminded his brother to be discreet.

"What do you think, do they look like relatives or friends?" Asked Seung Ho quietly, keeping his gaze at his brother.

"Well, the young lady didn't look like a city girl, judging by the look of her attire, I'm quite sure she is from the countryside…hmm…maybe she's a cousin or niece." Seung Jae came up with a plausible scenario. Then he whispered to Seung Ho, "I saw him threw a brochure into a rubbish bin earlier on, should we go pick it up?"

"All right, let's check it out." The adventure sounded exciting, Seung Ho supported his brother's idea instantly.

When Young-tae and Suk-mi went down the escalator and exited the building, Seung Jae went to the rubbish bin and picked up the brochure Young-tae discarded earlier on. Seung Ho followed behind, stood next to him to shield him from the passers-by. They looked at the brochure and found the name of the bakery training school.

"So they've gone to register for a course with this bakery training school…I see, maybe the girl is a relative, he was helping her with the enrolment of the course." That was Seung Jae's conclusion.

"Forget it, it's nothing serious, she's a relative who needed his help, that's all. Can we go shop for Hyuk's birthday present?" Seung Ho became impatient when they did not find anything out of the ordinary from the brochure.

"All right, let's go." Though there were lingering doubts, Seung Jae threw the brochure back into the rubbish bin and went on with their shopping trip.

A Budding Friendship

A few days after they coincidentally met Young-tae at the shopping mall, Seung Jae was still troubled by a nagging voice in his head, he decided to pay Rui-a a visit after work. He did not inform her of his visit in advance for fear she might come up with an excuse not to see him.

"Miss Rui-a!" Seung Jae went forward to Rui-a as soon as he saw her coming out of the lift.

"Mr Seung Jae…it's nice to see you again." Rui-a was surprised to see him at her office building.

"I've a meeting with some clients nearby, since your office is around this area, I thought I should drop by to see you. Are you heading home? Care to join me for dinner?" Seung Jae was hoping he could get some information from Rui-a about Young-tae.

"Hmm…I'm actually heading home for dinner with my family. Do you have something important to discuss with me?" Rui-a thought that there should not be anything important or urgent for him to visit her.

"No, just to have dinner with you, since you treated me to dinner last month, I thought maybe I should return the treat. Well, I've waited for close to an hour, perhaps you could make my wait worthwhile?" Seung Jae persuaded her with a justifiable excuse.

"Well, I didn't ask you to wait for me in the first place, the next time you should just give me a call to say you're nearby. All right then, I'll have dinner with you, let me call my mom first." Rui-a seemed uncomfortable with his sudden visit, but she agreed to have dinner with him since it would be ill-mannered for her to ask him to leave.

"Should we go for western cuisine?" Seung Jae asked Rui-a cautiously, observing her facial expression, he was relieved she was not really angry with him.

"Fine with me, since you're paying." Rui-a was trying to be polite, but her reply turned out to be rather monotonous.

They went to a western restaurant in a hotel, it was spacious with few diners, a place suitable for a good conversation.

"So what have you been doing these few days?" Seung Jae started the conversation with daily activities.

"I'm always working, I don't know, I'm feeling tired nowadays, the thought of being not suitable in the job kept bothering me. How was your week?" For Rui-a, it was a time to unwind, she certainly would not like to talk about work.

"I had a rough time last week, a client was making noise about a delay in the construction of a property project, we might need to come up with some sort of compensation. Sorry, I should leave business matters out of the conversation. Anyway, how's your boyfriend, is he a full-time painter?" Seung Jae went straight to the matter he was interested in.

"He's a senior finance executive in a bank, he has been painting for years. Last month's exhibition was his debut as an amateur painter. Actually, we're getting married next Spring." Since they were chatting about the daily life, Rui-a thought it was appropriate to let Seung Jae know about the wedding, hopefully he would stop wasting time on her.

"I see, congratulations." Seung Jae's heart sank upon hearing her impending wedding, but he forced a smile on his face, he then continued with the conversation, "So you've been together for a long time?"

"Yes, we're from the same town, we knew each other for two decades and we're together for ten years." Rui-a recounted the number of years of their relationship.

"That's a long time…" Seung Jae's heart sank deeper as he felt it was impossible to win her heart based on the fact that they had a decade long relationship and they were getting married in a few months' time.

"Your boyfriend is really talented, has he been painting for a long time?" A disheartened Seung Jae shifted the focus of the conversation on Young-tae.

"He has been painting for about seven years now, he used to take short courses in the evening to learn painting. Last month's exhibition was his first, thanks for buying one of his paintings." Rui-a was proud when talking about Young-tae.

"I see, his landscape paintings are extremely varied, I mean, he could paint a vast variety of different natural scenery, like waterfall, seascape, pine tree forest, river stream, etc. I'm really impressed." Seung Jae gave a positive review for Young-tae's paintings.

"It feels great to hear such a compliment. He has a strong passion in landscape painting and often took trips to do outdoor painting on islands." Rui-a appreciated Seung Jae's flattering remark, she was convinced that Seung Jae was a connoisseur in paintings. She then added, "I guess he enjoys his painting trips because he could get away from the hustle and bustle of the city life. However, that does not mean working in the office was a chore to him, he's very devoted to his banking job." Rui-a talked about her boyfriend in a sweet and delicate manner.

A short while later, the main course was served. Seung Jae and Rui-a carried on with their conversation as they began to savour their food.

"He seems to be a perfect person, is that how he is in your mind?" Seung Jae was rather anxious as he had not gotten any 'valuable' information yet.

"Hmm...he is far from being perfect." Rui-a blurted a surprising answer, she herself was taken aback by the way she valued her boyfriend, "Sorry, I mean he's only a human being, he can't be perfect, you see, I love him for who he is, it's not about perfection." Rui-a thought she should be prudent when talking about Young-tae's life experience, as such, she did not mention he sought consultation from a psychiatrist regularly.

"Are you two really on good terms? You've been out for a few hours but he didn't call, I'm just curious." Seung Jae delved into their relationship.

"Actually, my mom and younger sis are at my boyfriend's apartment these few weeks, we keep him company because he was injured in an accident during a trip to Ganghwado." Rui-a clarified readily so as not to give him the idea that there was any problem in their relationship.

"He has relatives on the island? Was he seriously injured?" Seung Jae probed further.

"He doesn't have relatives on Ganghwado, he was there to paint. It was a robbery, someone attacked him from behind. He suffered a minor fracture on his neck, and he has to wear a neck brace." Rui-a briefly described the attack in the mountain.

"So you've a younger sister, what profession is she in?" After determining Young-tae was the person he saw at the shopping mall, and that he did not have relatives on the island, Seung Jae needed to determine who was with him the other day.

"My sister is a high school student. Do you have any siblings?" Asked Rui-a out of curiosity.

"Yes, I'm the eldest and I've two younger brothers." Thought Seung Jae, the young lady he saw the other day did not look like a city girl, "Nowadays, a lot of young girls like to keep long and straight hair, does your sister keeps long hair as well." Seung Jae thought it was not the right time to tell her he saw Young-tae with a young lady just a few days ago, what if she did not know the young lady at all?

"My sister likes to keep shoulder-length hair and tie it in a ponytail with a ribbon, she does it wherever she goes." Replied Rui-a, she was feeling strange as to how the conversation had developed.

"I see..." Seung Jae was very sure the young lady had long hair and she did not tie it up.

"Is there another artist in his family?" Seung Jae tried to get more details of Young-tae's family background.

"He's the only child to his parents. I have some relatives in the old neighbourhood, so does he, I'm quite sure there isn't any other artist in his family." Said Rui-a in a casual manner.

Seung Jae paused for a while, then he switched subject, "It must be very uncomfortable wearing a neck brace, I suppose?"

"It's really inconvenient, he had to be careful not to dampen the neck brace during showers, if his neck gets itchy, he would use a chopstick to scratch it. The only good thing is he is able to take a break from work." Said Rui-a, she seemed to enjoy the food as well as the conversation.

"I'm sure he could go out door for some fresh air if he feels bored at home." Seung Jae tried to direct the conversation to his activities during his recovery.

"That's right, it's hard to stay indoor for a long period of time, last week he went to the supermarket with my mom and sister, a few days ago he had to send his laptop for repair." Rui-a thought it did not matter whether he stayed indoor or outdoor.

"Repair shops don't open on weekends, right?" At this point, Seung Jae felt tense inside as he was worried the irrelevance of his query might sound strange to Rui-a.

"Let me see, I think he went out on Tuesday." Rui-a found it rather odd how the conversation had developed. Then it struck her that she had to fetch her mother and sister home from Young-tae's apartment.

"It's getting late, I need to make a move now. It's really nice chatting with you, and thanks for the wonderful dinner." Said Rui-a as she took a glimpse at her watch.

"Don't stand on ceremony. Can I give you a lift?" Said Seung Jae as he raised his hand to signal to a waiter for his bill.

"I'm driving today, thank you." Rui-a thanked Seung Jae again, smiling with pleasure, she seemed to enjoy the evening with Seung Jae.

They left the restaurant after Seung Jae settled the bill, and headed back to the office building where they parked their cars.

When Seung Jae came home, he went around the house looking for Seung Ho, and found his brother in the study room reading a magazine.

"Ho, the neck brace painter we saw on Tuesday, he told his girlfriend he was sending his laptop for repair, something is not right, he was keeping things from his girlfriend." Seung Ho disclosed what he heard from Rui-a to his brother.

"Who told you? You know his girlfriend?" Seung Ho was puzzled where and how his brother got the information.

"I just had dinner with his girlfriend." Seung Jae told his brother about having dinner with Rui-a.

"Are you interested in the girlfriend? No wonder you're so keen on the matter." Seung Ho snickered at his brother, "Don't waste time on someone else's girlfriend, for goodness sake."

"It's not what you think, don't you think something is amiss? This person brought Min-hye to the national park, and he brought a young lady to register for a bakery course, you don't find it strange?" Seung Jae raised a reasonable doubt.

"The young lady could be his relative or sister, and what can he do with Min-hye in a touristed park?" Seung Ho gave a rational assumption.

"According to his girlfriend, he doesn't have relatives on Ganghwado, and he's the only child. That is to say, he and the young lady are not related if the young lady is from Ganghwado. The fact that he was injured on Ganghwado might be related to this young lady as well. The point is, if he was helping a relative he did not have to lie to his girlfriend, right?" Seung Jae analysed the situation with dedication.

"Maybe his girlfriend knew about the enrolment but she didn't think there's a need to tell you, after all, it's their family affair. It's possible that he sent his laptop for repair before he went to the cooking school, so he was not lying at all." Seung Ho came up with a justifiable scenario, although he too had an inkling there might be something wrong with the tutor's behaviour.

"That's possible, maybe I'm being too suspicious." Seung Jae accepted his brother's presumption.

"I think you're having a serious crush with his girlfriend, so much so that you are finding fault with the boyfriend. By the way, do you still want to go skiing next week?" Seung Ho repudiated his brother's suspicion with the suggestion that he was infatuated with the girlfriend. On the other hand, he was thinking is there any likelihood that Min-hye would fall for her tutor?

"Yes, we'll go skiing next week...something is not right somewhere...what is it?" The obscurity of the occurrences was still bugging Seung Jae.

Chp 6

◆

Trilogy of Paintings

Young-tae had his neck brace removed at the hospital four weeks later, he resumed work thereafter. His colleagues welcomed him back with a dinner treat the first day he returned to work. A few days later, he returned to Dr Kang's clinic to continue his therapy sessions.

"Good to see you again Young-tae, did you enjoy your debut exhibition?" As Dr Kang was impressed by Young-tae's paintings, he anticipated some sort of a good result at the end of the exhibition.

"It's a phenomenal experience for me, I was totally overwhelmed from the start till the end of the event. A total of seven of my paintings were sold at the end of the exhibition, I was thrilled. The manager of the gallery has indicated that he would showcase my paintings at least once a year at his gallery, hence, I've to be more vigilant and put in a conscientious effort in my painting from now on." Young-tae was certain that he would be taking his painting activities more seriously in future.

"That's really an extraordinary achievement, congratulations. I'm glad you're propelling yourself toward a promising direction, it's remarkable." Dr Kang endorsed his success and positive attitude wholeheartedly.

"I really appreciate your encouragement." Young-tae was touched by Dr Kang's moral support.

"It's winter time, I assume you don't do outdoor painting, so I'm going to give you a piece of homework, to do painting at your apartment." A piece of work in which Dr Kang believed would benefit Young-tae's therapy.

"What kind of work do you wish me to paint?" Young-tae was curious about the unexpected mission.

"I'm sure the unfortunate event where you and your girlfriend Eun-ja encountered during a hurricane back in your home town was still vivid to you, I need you to paint the accident into pictures. It could be a trilogy whereby you re-enact the accident and express your feelings from the beginning to the end of the accident." Dr Kang set forth his idea while assigning the work to Young-tae.

"Oh that…" The unexpected assignment caused some hesitation in Young-tae.

"Are you feeling uncomfortable with the idea? Is't too hard to reproduce the tragedy on your canvas? Or you don't wish your personal affair to be visible in public?" Dr Kang raised several questions to elicit his response.

"I'll try." The new task had stupefied Young-tae, he was since consumed in deep thoughts. Was he able to revisit the tragedy and prominently paint it out on the canvas? Was he able to exhibit such a painting in public? He was perplexed as he doubted himself whether he had the mental strength to complete the task.

"It was like telling a story, in your first picture, the weather was amiable, both of you were climbing the tree or on a tree branch, the second picture shows the hurricane swept both of you off balance, and the third picture, Eun-ja was lying motionless on the riverbank with you next to her. What do you think of the arrangement?" Dr Kang suggested how he could paint the story in a trilogy.

"It's fine." Young-tae suffered an intense feeling of wretchedness, his voice was subdued and his tone dried as dust.

"As soon as you've completed the trilogy, discuss with the gallery manager to have your paintings exhibited for sale." Dr Kang further suggested this idea to Young-tae.

"I'm against this idea, I don't wish to share my private experience with the public." The idea of displaying the heart wrenching tragedy in public was out of the question for Young-tae.

"Please explain why you're against this idea, the tragedy happened two decades ago, by now the feeling of sorrow and guilt should not be intense anymore?" An upset Dr Kang queried Young-tae's state of mind.

"I mean…it's too private an affair to me, I don't wish to tell everybody I've such an unfortunate experience, especially when I'm partly responsible for the tragedy, I'm ashamed to let the public know about it." Young-tae disclosed his true feeling about this matter.

"Nobody would hold you responsible for the tragedy, it was an accident, you should bear this in mind." Dr Kang was perturbed that after two decades Young-tae's feeling of guilt and shame was still intense.

"Furthermore, I shouldn't earn profit or sympathy out of my story, artists should not promote their works with such intention." Young-tae came forth with the standpoint of an idealistic artist.

"You know what, your personal experience tells people who you are, it does not determine whether how good your paintings are, in other words, people purchase your paintings because they value them as masterpieces, they don't buy your paintings because of your tragedy. Your personal experience can be incorporated in your paintings, and it became a unique style of yours, other artists could never be able to emulate such experience in their works. Do you get what I mean?" Dr Kang persuaded him with intense conviction.

"I get what you mean." Replied Young-tae as he gradually assimilated himself with Dr Kang's point of view.

"I'm glad you see my point, let's take a break." Dr Kang then went out of his office, and returned shortly with two cups of tea. They sipped on their tea and carried on with their conversation.

"You appear to have put on weight, tell me what you did in the past few weeks." Since Young-tae stepped into his office, Dr Kang noticed Young-tae's face was more rounded than before.

"After the exhibition, I took a trip to Ganghwado, went up the mountain to paint the panoramic view of the seascape. Shortly after I began painting, a robber attacked me from behind and I sustained injuries on my neck and back, and have to stay home for a month. I suffered a minor cervical fracture and was wearing a neck brace for a month. Rui-a's mom took care of my three meals every day, it's hard not to put on some weight." Young-tae told him about the 'robbery' on Ganghwa Island, and how he gained weight.

"So you've met with an unfortunate event, sorry to hear that. Rui-a's mom took care of you in such dedication, I'm green with envy." Dr Kang commented his experience with a perky remark.

"Yes, I'm really fortunate to have known Rui-a's family. By the way, I'm getting married next Spring." Young-tae told Dr Kang about his impending marriage.

"That's great, congratulations! I can imagine you'll be well taken care of by Rui-a's family, just be careful not to put on any more weight..ha…ha" Quipped Dr Kang, exuding the jovial side of his persona.

"I'll be more mindful of my diet in future." Smiled Young-tae in the light-hearted atmosphere.

Year-end Appraisal

A few weeks after Young-tae resumed work, Mr Kim, the manager of the HyungDai bank where Young-tae worked in, called for a meeting for all the staff when they finished work at the end of the day.

"I'm pleased to announce to you that most of you have performed well in the past year, the letter of increment and promotion will be given to you next week. As you know we are opening a new branch at the Komax Shopping Mall in March, some of you will be transferred to manage and assist in the operations of the new branch. Those who are transferred will likely be involved in the recruitment of the new staff for the branch." Mr Kim paused for a moment for his subordinates to raise questions.

"Mr Joo (Young-tae), Mr Lee, Mr Baek, Mr Oh, Ms Yi and Ms Han will be transferred to the new branch. Do you have any query or opinion before I end this meeting?" As Mr Kim announced the list of staff to be transferred to the new branch, swishing whispers began to fill the meeting room.

"I would like to have a short meeting with the six staff who will be transferred to the new branch, the rest of you can leave the meeting room." The employees who were not involved in the reshuffling left the meeting room while Mr Kim and the six staff stayed behind.

"Actually, your transfer comes with a promotion, so I congratulate all of you here. Is there anyone here who doesn't wish to go to the new branch?" Mr Kim gave his staff a chance to voice out any objection, but none of them spoke up.

"Well then, in the new branch, Mr Joo will be the manager overseeing the entire operations, Mr Lee will be the assistant manager, Mr Baek and Mr Oh will supervise the finance team, and Ms Yi and Ms Han will supervise the bank tellers. As for me, I've been promoted to become the general manager of the bank, and I'll visit the new branch at least once a week." After announcing the new positions to the transferred staff, Mr Kim revealed his own promotion. The faces of all the staff in the room were beaming with pride and gratification.

"Congratulations on your promotion, Mr Kim." Mr Lee was first to convey his well wishes. The rest followed suit to congratulate him.

"Young-tae, you'll be leading this group of colleagues, all of you will receive the formal letter of transfer sometime next week. Starting next week, you can conduct interviews to recruit new staff for the branch, and make sure that everything is in place at the new office, such as the furniture and stationery, and so on. You're to report to me directly for all matters big and small regarding the new branch." Mr Kim instructed Young-tae some basic duties he had to carry out prior to the opening of the new branch.

"Yes, Mr Kim." Young-tae listened to his instructions attentively, at the same time, he was trying hard to fathom how he landed himself in such a crucial position as he had heard earlier it was to be filled by another colleague.

"All right, I need to have a few words with Young-tae, the rest of you can leave the meeting room." Mr Kim asked Young-tae to stay behind for a private discussion.

"Mr Kim, I heard this post is supposed to be taken up by Mr Park, why is there a change?" Young-tae inquired when the other colleagues had left the meeting room.

"I received the news last week. Do you know Mr Choi Myung-hwan, one of the members of our board of director?" To Mr Kim's knowledge, Young-tae did not have any relatives or friends sitting on the board.

"Mr Choi...Mr Choi Myung-hwan...hmm...is he Min-hye's father? Yes, Mr Choi is the father of my tuition student." Young-tae had no idea Min-hye's father was one of the bank's directors.

"I see, the management had a meeting with the directors last week, Mr Choi spoke highly of you and suggested the post should go to you, I guess the management was influenced by his commendation." Mr Kim disclosed a piece of information of the closed door meeting.

"I was his daughter's Mathematics tutor, I suppose he was satisfied that I've helped his daughter in achieving good grades in school." He landed the job because Min-hye's father put in a few good words for him during the board meeting, Young-tae thought. Then he asked Mr Kim, "Have you spoken to Mr Park about this?" Young-tae thought he might offend Mr Park by taking up the post.

"Don't worry about Mr Park, he's promoted as well, he might be assisting me in the near future. Let's go for dinner." Mr Kim and Young-tae had a cordial work relationship since Young-tae joined the bank. Very soon Young-tae would become a manager, this was a time to tighten their relationship and take it to a higher level.

Heading home to his apartment after dinner with Mr Kim, Young-tae felt his body was warm from head to toe in the cool windy night. Deep in his thoughts, Young-tae hoped Eun-ja would be pleased with his promotion as he had done an excellent job in fulfilling her aspiration. If Eun-ja was alive, there would be no regrets in their lives. He blamed himself for not being able to protect Eun-ja during the hurricane, his heart was filled with sorrow, his eyes swelled and tears flew under the dark gloomy sky.

The new position and office had seen Young-tae spending most of his time meeting with his co-workers, interviewing candidates, planning work flow, solving problems, so on and so forth. After slogging away for more than a month, he really needed to take a break. It was winter, and the weather was freezing, it was not really a suitable time for a painting trip. Nevertheless, he applied for a few days off from work. He gave Rui-a a call before he took his trip.

"Rui-a, I'll be taking a trip to Ulleungdo to take some photos of winter scenery, I'll be back in a few days' time." Young-tae told Rui-a about his impending trip.

"It's so cold out there, and Ulleungdo is far away, can you stay in-door and make arrangements for our wedding ceremony?" Rui-a was not agreeable with his trip as there were still works to be done for their wedding ceremony.

"I'll meet the wedding planner again to finalise the flow of the ceremony and the guest list before I leave for the island, is there anything else you want me to do?" Young-tae had planned to tie up some loose ends before he took his trip.

"All right, just don't go hiking in the mountain in this weather, the ground is slippery, and remember to bring your down jacket with you. Call me when you're back." Rui-a was worried he might meet with some mishap again.

"Okay, I'll be careful." Young-tae was relieved Rui-a was not strongly against his trip.

After Young-tae called up the wedding planner and made an appointment in the afternoon, he gave Min-hye a call.

"Min-hye, it's me, would your parents be at home this evening? I would like to pay them a visit." Young-tae called to check whether Min-hye's parents were at home.

"Teacher, please hold the line, I'll check with my mom." Min-hye went to the living room to ask Mrs Choi whether they would be at home that day.

"Teacher, my parents will be at home tonight, what time are you coming?" Asked Min-hye for the visiting time.

"Is 8pm a convenient time?" Enquired Young-tae.

"Yes. May I know the reason for your visit?" Min-hye enquired politely.

"I've been promoted to become a branch manager recently, I heard your dad put in good words for me during a board meeting, so I wish to visit him today to thank him in person." Young-tae told Min-hye about his promotion.

"I see, that's cool! Congratulations." A cheery Min-hye was happy for her tutor's promotion.

"You know, I can't do it without you putting in hard work in your studies, your dad was satisfied with my performance because of your good grades, I've to thank you in person too." Young-tae spoke with sincerity, his tone was rather serious.

"Really, ha…ha…" Young-tae's compliment had made Min-hye giggling delightfully at the other end of the phone, she was amazed that her father would intervene in her tutor's promotion.

"All right, I'll see you tonight. Bye bye." Young-tae hung up the phone, smiling heartily as it was a pleasure to hear Min-hye's bubbly voice again.

After he had done with meeting his wedding planner, Young-tae bought a bottle of liquor, nicely wrapped for Mr Choi, and a bouquet of flowers for the ladies in the house. He arrived at the Choi mansion and was welcomed by Min-hye at the front door. Mr and Mrs Choi were at the living room watching TV.

"Good evening, Mr Choi, Mrs Choi." Young-tae greeted Min-hye's parents and sat on the sofa when Mr Choi gesturing at him to take a seat. He put the gifts on the table in front of the sofa.

"Young-tae, about your promotion, I didn't do much, the decision was made by the management as a whole, so you should give yourself credit for clinching the post." As a respectable businessman, Mr Choi was benevolent in that he had influenced Young-tae's promotion but did not take full credit for it, in addition, he commended Young-tae for his own capabilities.

"Thank you, I really appreciate your kindness, I'll remember your benevolence by heart." Young-tae bowed his head slightly to show his heartfelt gratitude to Mr Choi.

"Supposed you encounter any problem in your new position, you've to discuss it with your superior. There would be some problems here and there, spend some time to listen to the superior who are more experienced than you. All in all, I'm sure you'll do a good job, have faith in yourself." Encouraged Mr Choi, he was like a concerned elderly to Young-tae.

"I'll keep that in mind, thank you for the advice." Young-tae nodded with sincerity, he regarded Mr Choi with great respect and reverence.

"Min-hye will be doing her high school education starting next year, please help her out if she encounters any problems with her school work." Mr Choi pleaded with Young-tae for his mentorship.

"I'll help her out if there's a need, but I feel she can do well on her own since she had established a strong foundation in the past year." Young-tae reaffirmed Min-hye's performance to Mr Choi.

Mr Choi was contented with his daughter's performance in school as well as Young-tae's dedication. They chatted for about half an hour before Young-tae took his leave. Min-hye accompanied him to the gate.

"Teacher, since I won't be seeing you again, can I call you up just to chit chat?" Asked Min-hye, hoping that she could keep in touch with Young-tae in future.

"Call me up if you feel bored, but don't neglect your study." Reminded Young-tae, as he had confident Min-hye had become more mature and independent, and that she could study on her own.

"Actually, you still owe me an island trip, since you won't be tutoring me anymore, can you bring me on an island trip as a farewell trip for us?" Min-hye remembered the island trip they talked about several months ago.

"I took you to the national park, remember?" Young-tae thought he had settled the issue earlier on.

"No…national park is not an island, I'll have lots of fun on an island, please…" Min-hye held his hand and shook slightly, pestering him with her imploring eyes.

"All right then, I'll bring you to one when the winter is over." Young-tae gave in to her request, he patted her shoulder and left the mansion. Min-hye appeared upbeat when Young-tae agreed to her request. She was elated to have earned a trip with her tutor, whom she yearned for his affectionate attention.

Up on the Lighthouse

To visit the Ulleung Island, Young-tae took several hours of bus ride to Mukho ferry terminal in the evening, he stayed a night near the terminal so as to take a ferry ride in the morning to the Ulleung Island.

The ferry ride took about three hours, Young-tae dozed off most of the time throughout the journey. As Young-tae got off the ferry, there were very few tourists on the island, he went to one of the guest houses to rent a room to stay for a night.

After taking lunch in a local eatery, Young-tae roamed around the island taking photos randomly. The island was tranquil in the frigid weather. He strode watchfully along the coastal area, enjoying the wonderful nature the creator of the universe had bestowed on mother earth. There were seagulls gliding above the blue ocean, the sounds of the seagulls and the beating waves were soothing music to his mind and body.

He returned from his coastal walk feeling refreshed, and decided to visit the lighthouse standing in a distance. A lighthouse provides guidance for maritime navigation, perhaps he could attain some inspiration from it. It was a time when he was experiencing exceptional transformation in his life, was he able to strive and survive in the new endeavours?

Young-tae climbed up to the viewing deck of the lighthouse, after taking some photos with his camera, he paused to take in the sublime beauty of the horizon. As his gaze drifted along the horizon, he saw Eun-ja's face smiling at him from a distance. Eun-ja's image was like a reflection in the water, floating in the greyish blue sky.

"Eun-ja…are you here for me? I know you're safeguarding me all the while." Younga-tae kneeled on the deck, his hands holding on to the railings, his eyes fixed on the image of Eun-ja.

"Eun-ja…do you know I've fulfilled your dream… yes, I'm doing it for you to keep you alive in my heart… Eun-ja, I'm sorry for not being able to protect you during the hurricane…if heaven allows, I would trade my life for yours." In a confession of guilt, Young-tae's tears streamed down his face as he spoke to Eun-ja.

"I'm sorry, I'm really sorry…I've been living a smooth and happy life since you left me. Deep down, I've been waiting for a mishap to befall on me so that I could rise to heaven and be with you again…" A guilt-ridden Young-tae repeatedly blamed himself for her death. The weather was gloomy, so was he.

"Look at me now, I'm doing well, achieving success at work and paintings, but you're not here for me, how am I supposed to carry on living this happy life without you?" The grief-stricken Young-tae continued to pour his heart out to Eun-ja.

"Eun-ja…I'll be getting married to your cousin, Rui-a. I don't know why I can't feel the blissful joy, it's so unfair to her….what am I supposed to do…she was so devoted and loyal to me, I don't deserve her love at all." Young-tae's voice was getting dreary, his eyes reddish and his body feeble.

"What am I supposed to do…Eun-ja…" Young-tae gazed at Eun-ja and said, "If I end my life here and now, would you forgive me?" Eun-ja's image vanished in an instant as Young-tae sought for her forgiveness by suggesting taking his own life. Young-tae was distressed and terrified, he sat on the viewing deck feeling desolate and dispirited, his legs were numb and his mind went blank, he looked like a piece of wreckage strewn over the beach by the sea wave.

Feeling weak and depressed after his intense dialogue with Eun-ja on the lighthouse, Young-tae dragged himself back to the town area, he bought some food and a few bottles of wine before he went back to the guest house.

While he was eating the meal, which consisted of squids, assorted vegetables, and rice, he recalled that squids and seafood were his father's favourite food. Just then, tears dripped onto the food he was eating. During the despondent state shortly after Eun-ja passed away, his father had once reprimanded him for being too weak in handling Eun-ja's death, and that if Young-tae should decide to take his own life, his father would never forgive him.

He drank the wine one bottle after another to drown his sorrow, and soon he was drunk and fell asleep with his face covered in tears.

Chp 7

◆

Trilogy Exhibited

Back from Ulleung Island, Young-tae embarked on the task of painting the unfortunate incident which took away Eun-ja's life two decades ago. He was heavy hearted whenever he lifted his paint brush. Young-tae recalled the scenery of the day the tragedy struck, he carefully mixed the colours and sketched the details onto the canvas. With the tragedy being vivid till this date, the paintings were painted with utmost care and diligent. However, he went through the process at snail's pace, as he was often interrupted by his sorrow, and he had to try hard to break away the invisible shackles that were restraining his movements.

The most onerous part of the task was the last painting, in which he had to depict Eun-ja's body lying motionlessly on the riverbank, and he, prostrated on the ground next to her body crying helplessly. When he was painting Eun-ja's blood flowing into the river stream, he was too distraught and started crying convulsively. True enough, as the portrayal of the tragic incident was completed, he felt a great deal of inner tension had been released.

He took a photo of the completed trilogy and showed it to the gallery manager to negotiate for them to be exhibited at the gallery. Rui-a was at the meeting and helped explained the tragedy to the manager. Moved by the unfortunate event, the manager agreed to have the trilogy exhibited at the gallery for one month.

"Ms Rui-a, it's me again, do you have any appointment after work today? Care to have dinner with me?" Seung Jae, reminiscing the wonderful time he spent with Rui-a over dinner last month, tried his luck again to ask Rui-a out for dinner.

"Mr Seung Jae, good evening. It's good to hear from you again. I'm going over to the gallery after work, would you like to join me?" Rui-a took the opportunity to invite Seung Jae to the gallery to view her boyfriend's trilogy.

"Sure, is your boyfriend's painting being exhibited again?" Seung Jae did not think Rui-a invited him over to the gallery without a purpose.

"Yes, but this time round only a set of three paintings are showcased, it's an unique trilogy, care to join me at the gallery?" Rui-a would promote Young-tae's paintings to anyone, especially when Seung Jae was a potential customer.

"Would you have dinner with me after that?" Seung Jae's request sounded like a business deal.

"All right, I'll see you at the gallery around 7pm." Rui-a was not offended by his request, in fact she had developed a fondness for Seung Jae, who had agreed to view Young-tae's paintings with good grace.

At the gallery, Rui-a narrated the story of the trilogy to Seung Jae with much dedication. A heart-breaking tragedy depicted in the tranquility of the countryside, was awe-inspiring to Seung Jae. At the same time, the reason behind the painter's melancholic appearance had since come to light with the trilogy.

During dinner, Seung Jae had a heartfelt talk with Rui-a concerning the trilogy.

"It's such an unfortunate event, I wonder how Mr Joo pulled through the mournful period after his young girlfriend passed away." Said Seung Jae, whose sullen look suggested he was deeply moved by the tragedy.

"Eun-ja was my cousin, I too was devastated when she passed away. At that time, Young-tae could not concentrate on his studies, he gave up schooling and toiled in the farms all day long. Fortunately, he went back to school the next year, and was able to carry on with his studies without much problem." Rui-a recalled the tough period Young-tae went through after her cousin passed away.

"His fighting spirit was admirable. By the way, it's an unique idea to portray the tragedy in paintings, and I do feel the value of this type of paintings would rise sharply over time, however, I have not thought of a suitable place to display the trilogy, at the moment, I still prefer landscape paintings. Nevertheless, I'm sure this trilogy would be well loved and coveted by some avid collectors." Seung Jae perceived highly of the trilogy and explained his regrets for not purchasing the paintings.

"Don't worry about it, I'm contented that you are willing to spend some time viewing and commenting on it." Although Seung Jae did not purchase the trilogy, Rui-a was pleased that he spoke highly of it.

When he came back home, Seung Jae's parents were watching TV in the sitting room, he greeted them and went to look for Seung Ho at the study room to discuss what he heard from Rui-a.

"Ho, I heard something about the painter today." Seung Jae waited for Seung Ho to put aside his story book, he continued, "Something tragic happened to him when he was 16 years old."

"What was it?" The word 'tragic' had raised Seung Ho's curiosity, he became interested with what Seung Jae was about to disclose.

"One afternoon after school, he and his 16 year-old girlfriend met with a hurricane when they were climbing up a tree, they were swept off balance and fell to a riverbank, he suffered a concussion but her head was slammed onto a rock and she died of profuse bleeding." The atmosphere was sombre as Seung Jae gave a brief account of the tragedy.

"So you have dinner with his girlfriend again?" Seung Ho was puzzled why his brother was so persistent about the matter. Then he said, "It's an unfortunate tragedy, but I don't see a linkage between this and the tutor's young female companion at the shopping mall."

"There were experts who reported that some psychopaths who commit crimes in their adulthood suffered ill-treatment or traumatized experience when they were young. Perhaps, a part of the painter was seeking solace in young females, or he's trying to relive the happy moments he had with his deceased girlfriend." Seung Jae came up with some psychological analysis.

"Are you suggesting he befriends young girls with an ulterior motive?" As Seung Ho raised his query, he was disgusted by such scandalized behaviour.

"Don't you think it's possible? Remember the facts that he brought Min-hye to a national park without your knowledge, and he enrolled the young lady to a bakery course without telling his girlfriend? Something is not right." Seung Jae suspected Young-tae might have engaged in intimate affairs with some young girls, but since Min-hye was his teenage brother's girlfriend, he did not wish to distraught him with explicit descriptions, after all it was just his speculations.

"Ho, I'm sure the bakery course has started in the new year, go and find out which day and what time does the young lady takes her course." Seung Jae gave an instruction to his brother.

"What are you going to do after I get the information?" Seung Ho was curious what his brother would do next.

"We need to determine whether she's a relative or a friend, we'll need to know where she stays. What if she isn't a relative and they are living together? His girlfriend wouldn't know because he lives alone in his own apartment." Speaking like a private investigator, he put his hands on Seung Ho's shoulder.

"What if we found nothing? I don't want to waste my time on this." A reluctant Seung Ho was unwilling to do something ridiculous, such as acting like a private investigator or a policeman tracking down suspects.

"I promise if we found out that she's a relative, I'll not pursue the matter any further. For now, I need your cooperation, is that okay?" Seung Jae pleaded with his brother, who had remained dubious about the whole matter.

"All right then, don't forget your promise." Seung Ho agreed with his brother and reminded him not to pursue the matter if the young lady was a relative of Min-hye's tutor.

A Friend Indeed

To be as inconspicuous as possible while following behind the young lady, Seung Jae borrowed an old car from a friend, he put on his running attire, wore a pair of sunglasses and glued a moustache above his upper lip. As for Seung Ho, he put on some makeup and wore a dress borrowed from his mother. He also wore a wig and carried a compact mirror, which was to hide his face should the target become suspicious. They told their parents they were attending a costume party that evening.

"Jae, do you know where Min-hye's tutor lives?" Seung Ho asked his brother while they were waiting inside the car diagonally opposite the bakery school.

"Somewhere in Seoul. Keep an eye on the entrance of the training school, we can't afford to lose our target. Remember she has long straight hair." Seung Jae half covered his face with a magazine, his eyes fixated on the entrance of the school.

"Our target has just walked out of the school." Seung Ho saw Suk-mi and alerted Seung Jae. Anxiety built within them as they began their adventure.

"Keep your head as low as possible, where is she heading?" Seung Jae lowered his body while he got ready to start the vehicle.

"She crossed the road and....now she's at the bus stop." Seung Ho lowered his head and kept a watchful eye on Suk-mi.

Once Suk-mi boarded a bus, Seung Jae tailed behind the bus in a distance. They followed her all the way to Ganghwa Island, which was to their surprise, as they thought she would go to Young-tae's apartment. They drove pass her house as she entered the front door.

"Ho, should we go near the house and see what's happening inside the house?" Seung Jae parked the car at a distance away from Suk-mi's house.

"Since we're here, why not?" Seung Ho agreed with his brother and they got off the car, sneaking under the dark blue sky towards Suk-mi's house.

As the brothers were approaching Suk-mi's house, lo and behold, a big sturdy black hound started to bark ferociously at them, they got frightened out of their wits, turned their bodies around, and dashed as fast as they could to the car. Fortunately, the dutiful black hound was restrained by a leash, it could only bark but not chase after strangers.

After a short sprint back to the car, huffing and puffing and catching their breaths, Seung ho broke out a sweat and messed up the makeup on his face, while Seung Jae's moustache was half detached and covering his mouth. They burst into laughters when they saw each other's ludicrously funny appearances.

"Ho, Miss Rui-a, the painter's girlfriend, said he doesn't have any relative on this island, so this young lady is a friend." Said Seung Jae as he pulled off the moustache, and was ready to start the car engine.

"So they are friends, but we don't know anything else other than that." Replied Seung Ho, as he wiped the messy makeup off his face with a piece of tissue paper.

"If it's a clean friendship, the painter doesn't have to hide it from Miss Rui-a when he helped her enrol in a course in Seoul. The tricky part is, I can't just tell Miss Rui-a about this out of the blue, I also can't question the painter as he would not admit if there's any illicit behaviour between himself and the young lady." Seung Jae was perplexed by the thorny issue as he was sure there was something improper in the relationship.

"Luckily Min-hye won't be having tuition with him anymore, and she had also promised not to go out with him in future. I'm beginning to feel there's something odd about Min-hye's tutor." Said Seung Ho as Seung Jae started the car engine and they were ready to go back to Seoul.

"Well, hopefully she keeps her promise, I don't mean to discourage you, but you've to pay more attention on your relationship and be mindful of her behaviour." Seung Jae provided his point of view on his brother's relationship with Min-hye.

"All right. I'm hungry and tired, can we go for supper?" Seung Ho agreed with his brother.

"Okay, let's go for supper when we get back to Seoul." Replied Seung Jae as he contemplated how to continue with his 'investigation'.

"Min-hye, it's me, are you at home? What are you doing now?" Bothered by what they had just discovered, Seung Ho called up Min-hye.

"I'm at home surfing the internet, are you outside?" Min-hye thought she heard the swishing noises of passing vehicles on the road.

"I'm out with my brother, we're going for supper. Do you want to catch a movie this Saturday?" Seung Ho briefly reported his whereabouts, and asked her out for a movie.

"Okay, are you coming over to my place on Saturday?" Asked Min-hye as it was the usual routine for Seung Ho to go to her house before their outing.

"All right, I'll see you there on Saturday." Replied Seung Ho, who did not find any problem with Min-hye's attitude.

"Okay, see you. Bye." Replied Min-hye as she continued with internet surfing.

"Okay, bye." Seung Ho bade her goodbye and hung up the phone.

"Jae, Min-hye agreed to go for a movie this Saturday, thank goodness." The worries in Seung Ho's mind was gone, for he was sure Min-hye was faithful to their relationship.

"That's great, I'm happy for you." Replied Seung Jae as he pondered over what he could do next to find out more details about the painter's affairs.

Saturday Fever

On Saturday, Seung Ho waited for Min-hye outside the Choi mansion, when she came out of the mansion, Seung Ho gave her a little pink coloured teddy bear.

"This teddy bear is so adorable, it's really soft, thank you." Min-hye was overjoyed by Seung Ho's affectionate gesture, she received the gift and gave him a hug.

"I'm glad you like it." Beaming with a bright sunny smile, Seung Ho held her hand and they began their date on a pleasant note.

As they arrived at the cinema complex, they went to the ticket counter and joined the queue to buy movie tickets. Instead of waiting in the long queue, Seung Ho went away to buy some drinks and snacks.

"Ho, do you have any plan after the movie?" Min-hye asked Seung Ho when he came back with the drinks and snacks.

"We can go singing, or shopping, or to the arcade." An upbeat Seung Ho suggested a few activities.

"I feel like going for a roller coaster ride, do you want to go?" Min-hye told Seung Ho her preference.

"All right, we'll go to a theme park after the movie." Seung Ho agreed instantly, they bought the tickets when it was their turn and went into the movie theatre.

Whereas what was on Seung Jae's mind on this Saturday morning, when he was taking breakfast with his brothers, and later sent Seung Ho to Min-hye's house? He returned home after that, and he went out again, driving his friend's old car as he decided to visit the Ganghwa Island again.

Driving slowly around the island, he stopped the car near a row of local shops to get himself something to drink. Some middle-aged women were sitting on the ground in front of the shops hawking fresh vegetables.

"Good morning." Seung Jae smiled and greeted the women as he entered the provision shop to see what he could buy from there. He greeted the shop owner as well, browsed through the merchandise, and took a can of soda from the shelves. The female hawkers might be able to provide him with some local information, so he went out of the store and sat on the ground next to them. The female hawkers instantly recommended their fresh produce to him.

"Aunties, I was thinking maybe I should live here when I retire, sounds like a good idea." Seung Jae started the conversation with a casual topic. The ladies thought he was interested in their vegetables, did not show much enthusiasm in making a conversation with him.

"Young man, you can take your time to decide." Said one of the ladies, the rest burst into chuckles following her quick and humorous reply.

"I'm not sure is the island safe and secure to live in, that's all I wish to know." Seung Jae laughed slightly at her reply and continued with carrying out his mission of the day.

"The island is safe, there's not much to worry about security here." Said one of them.

"Aunties, I heard a robbery took place in the mountain a few months back, what happened? Do you know?" Enquired Seung Jae, hoping they might give him some details on the attack on Young-tae in the mountain.

"Robbery? Who would take the trouble to climb up the mountain to rob someone?" One of the ladies said. The rest whispering among each other, some names were mentioned in hushed tones.

"So it wasn't a robbery? I heard a painter was robbed." Speaking in a leisurely manner, Seung Jae took a gulp of soda and listened attentively.

"The painter was attacked and beaten by a local, but he's not after his money." One of the women said, not really willing to divulge what she knew.

"This painter loves the island and came here for outdoor painting, don't the people here welcome painters on the island?" Raising a question which might put the islanders in a bad light, Seung Jae could well get some genuine information with such tactic.

"It's not that, we welcome visitors on the island. The person who attacked the painter was jealous and angry because his girlfriend was in a relationship with the painter, it was the last straw when she wanted a breakup, so he beat him up to exact revenge on him." One of the ladies finally revealed the reason behind the attack.

"Wooh...the vegetables look fresh and nice, but you ladies' hearts are not very nice, what you do is to gather here and make up sensational stories as a past time." Seung Jae was in denial of the story so as to keep them talking.

"Ehh...you don't believe us? It's a triangle love affair gone bad, that's all." One of the ladies looked upon the incident in a light-hearted manner.

"This Suk-mi, she fell for the painter, but the painter only visited this island a few times a year, what kind of relationship can she hopes to develop?" Said another lady, who happened to live in Suk-mi's neighbourhood.

"Don't you think the attack was too brutal?" Seung Jae took another gulp of soda as he looked at the ladies, anxiously anticipated more details.

"I heard Suk-mi was intimately involved with the painter, she used this as the reason to break up with her boyfriend, that's why her boyfriend was so angry and beat up the painter." One of the ladies finally disclosed what Seung Jae was waiting to hear.

"Wooh...the painter and a young girl? Are you exaggerating?" Seung Jae was rather taken aback by the candid reply.

"That's the whole truth and nothing but the truth, Suk-mi had an intimate relationship with him." Said one of the women, she then pleaded with Seung Jae, "Keep Suk-mi's story to yourself, all right?" Seung Jae nodded and said, "I won't tell anybody."

"Young man, I got married when I was 16, and gave birth to my first child when I was 17. We don't make up story here." Another lady said matter-of-factly while providing Seung Jae her personal information and assured him the story was genuine.

"You want to buy vegetables or not?" Pointing at the vegetables, one of the ladies asked Seung Jae impatiently.

"Yes, yes, I'll buy them all, please wrap them up and carry them to my car over there. Thank you." Seung Jae bought all the vegetables and handed a sum of money to each of them. The female hawkers thought it was their luckiest day to have met such a generous visitor. They meticulously wrapped all the fresh produce and carried them to Seung Jae's car, they thanked Seung Jae and left in good spirits.

Driving back to Seoul, Seung Jae's heart was heavy, indeed, he was facing an unprecedented dilemma: if he told Rui-a the truth about her boyfriend, she would be devastated. What if she insisted on marrying her boyfriend even when she knew about his felony? On the other hand, if he did not tell her, it was unfair to her, as he believed she deserves someone better than a disgraceful lawbreaker.

Fundamentally, if she broke up with her boyfriend, he stood a good chance to win her heart over.

On this Saturday, Rui-a and Young-tae went to a jazz bar to celebrate Young-tae's promotion and the opening of the new branch. The music in the bar was loud, so they sat as far away from the stage as possible. The loving couple sipped on cocktails and whispered into each other's ears while they were entertained by the life performance.

The jazz bar was filled with romantic atmosphere, sweet and tender love songs warmed their hearts. Rui-a nestled up to Young-tae and rested her head on his shoulder, and Young-tae cuddled her closely to his chest. Regrettably, the romantic mood was interrupted by Rui-a's ringing phone.

"Rui-a, it's late, are you coming home soon?" It was Mdm Shim, she called to check what time her daughter was coming home.

"Mom, I'll be home soon, go to bed and don't wait up, Young-tae will send me home later." Replied Rui-a as she sat up straight to take the call.

"All right, don't stay out too late." Mdm Shim reminded her daughter, her voice sounded sleepy.

"Okay, I'm hanging up now." Said Rui-a as she hung up the phone.

"Should we go back now?" Mdm Shim's phone call reminded Young-tae that it was time to send Rui-a home.

"Can we stay a little longer, another half an hour?" Rui-a kept her phone and asked Young-tae.

"All right." Young-tae cuddled her body again and they continued to enjoy the saccharine music in the cozy atmosphere of the jazz bar.

By the time Young-tae sent Rui-a back to her house, the amorous couple were inseparable, they sneaked into Rui-a's room and luxuriated in a night of passionate intimacy.

Chp 8

◆

Fairyland

This was the Saturday Young-tae was supposed to bring Min-hye for an island trip. At daybreak, they met near Min-hye's house and took a taxi to the Incheon ferry terminal for a ferry ride to Deokjeokdo Island. Min-hye tied a pony tail, wore a windbreaker jacket, and slung a bag across her shoulder, she greeted Young-tae as 'brother Young-tae' instead of 'teacher' cheerily while she boarded a taxi with him.

On the ferry, Min-hye and Young-tae had some sushi rolls, prepared by Min-hye's domestic helper, for breakfast. It was a smooth and pleasant ride as there were not many passengers on the ferry. As the ferry arrived at the port of the island, they began their day trip by strolling along the street.

"Brother Young-tae, look, the morning mist is covering the town, what a beautiful sight, I feel like we have entered a fairyland, so magical!" Min-hye exclaimed with delight at the sight of the misty town, as she strolled along the street in a lively manner. Following with a short distance behind

Min-hye, Young-tae was deeply captivated by her youthful innocence and charm.

"Little fairy, do you want to go hiking in the mountain or playing along the beach?" Teased Young-tae.

"I don't have a magic wand, my magic wand is somewhere on the beach, which is where I should be heading." Min-hye was thinking of playing some games on the beach.

"All right, we'll go to the beach." A light-hearted Young-tae beaming with a smile on his face, as he enjoyed Min-hye's felicitous imagination.

At this juncture in Seoul, Seung Ho had made several phone calls to Min-hye, but she did not pick up her phone at all. After taking breakfast, Seung Jae went to Seung Ho's room and looked for him.

"What happened, Ho?" Seung Jae asked his youngest brother, who wore a morbid look on his face.

"Min-hye didn't pick up her phone, I've made several calls for an hour now." Bothered by Min-hye not picking up his calls, Seung Ho was thinking hard what could go wrong.

"You didn't plan earlier for an outing with her? Maybe she's still sleeping." A concerned Seung Jae was trying to allay his brother's anxiety.

"It's 9.20am, she doesn't sleep past 8.30am during weekends, she should be out of bed by now. I was too occupied with my school activities and didn't call her in the past week, what could she be doing?" Seung Ho thought he could ask her out in the morning for an outing in the afternoon.

"Do you have her house phone number?" Seung Jae prompted his brother to call her house instead.

"Yes." Seung Ho then called Min-hye's house phone number, and the domestic helper picked up the phone.

"Good morning, can I speak to Min-hye please?" It was the first time Seung Ho made a phone call to the Choi mansion.

"She's not at home." The domestic helper answered the call.

"May I know where did she go?" Asked Seung Ho.

"She went out for a picnic with some friends." Replied the domestic helper briefly.

"Do you know where is the picnic venue?" Seung Ho requested for information of her whereabouts.

"I'm sorry, I've no idea." Replied the domestic helper, in a monotonous tone again.

"Did anybody in the house know?" Asked Seung Ho anxiously, as he began to feel Min-hye was hiding something from him.

"Sorry, I've no idea. I'm hanging up the phone now." The domestic helper was not willing to disclose more details.

"Okay, thank you." Seung Ho hung up the phone, it did not make sense to him why Min-hye could not pick up phone calls while she was out for a picnic.

"Jae, Min-hye went out for a picnic with some friends, but why didn't she pick up the phone?" Seung Ho reported to his brother what the domestic helper told him.

"Do you know her friends?" Asked Seung Jae, trying to find a way to locate Min-hye's whereabouts.

"Not really, I don't have their phone numbers." Seung Ho was candid about his reply, at the same time he regretted for not knowing her closer friends.

"Well, to prevent our imagination from running wild, I'll check the painter's whereabouts with the girlfriend." Seung Jae said to his brother as he called up Rui-a.

"Good morning, Miss Rui-a, did I wake you up?" Seung Jae greeted Rui-a.

"Good morning, I'm out of bed for a while. That's early for you to call." Rui-a was wondering why Seung Jae called her up early in the morning.

"Oh…I was thinking of visiting the gallery later this afternoon, and meet up with Mr Joo for a friendly chat, do you know whether he would be available this afternoon?" Seung Jae made up an excuse that would not create any suspicion from Rui-a.

"He is not in town, I'm not sure what time he'd be back today." Replied Rui-a while going through some paper work.

"Oh…is he painting outdoor today? Where is he now?" Seung Jae was rather exasperated, and went straight to the point.

"It's his usual painting trip, he told me he's going to Deokjeokdo today." Rui-a disclosed Young-tae's whereabouts, and was puzzled why Seung Jae was looking for this information.

"What time he left for the island, do you know?" Seung Jae continued with his queries.

"It's off peak season, there are limited ferry rides, he probably took the morning ferry around 8am." Again Rui-a was perplexed why did Seung Jae need to know such details.

"Thank you, maybe I'll visit the gallery some other days. Bye bye." Seung Jae bade goodbye to Rui-a and hung up the phone.

"Ho, ask Min-hye's domestic helper what time Min-hye left the house this morning." Seung Jae told his brother to check the time Min-hye left for her picnic, hopefully he could find some clues from there. Seung Ho called the Choi mansion again, the domestic helper picked up the phone and they spoke briefly.

"The domestic helper said she left the house around 7am." Seung Ho reported to his brother.

"The painter took the 8am ferry, the timing would fit if they left the house around 7am. The problem is, we don't know whether they went out together." Seung Jae tried to keep calm, but he had a feeling they were out together, based on the findings he discovered from Ganghwa Island, which he had yet to find the right time to tell his teenage brother.

"They might be together, remember the last time she went out with him to the national park? She did not tell me until I bumped into them outside her house. If I didn't see them together, it's likely that she'd never tell me at all." Seung Ho analysed the situation based on the last incident.

"In that case, let's go to the ferry terminal and see whether we can find anything there." As Seung Jae made the decision, they double checked the location of the ferry terminal from the internet. Once the location was determined, they grabbed their jackets, phones and wallets, hopped in Seung Jae's car, and he drove toward the direction of the Incheon ferry terminal.

At the ferry terminal, Seung Ho showed Min-hye's picture on his handphone to the ticketing staff and asked them whether they had seen Min-hye boarded the morning ferry with a man. The ticketing staff was not sure but mentioned two persons matching their descriptions boarded the ferry that morning.

Seung Jae pleaded the ticketing staff to check whether Min-hye and Young-tae were on the passenger list, the staff reluctantly went through the booking system and gave them a positive answer.

Upon hearing the news, Seung Ho was exasperated, as on the journey to the ferry terminal, Seung Jae told him Young-tae had an intimate affair with the young lady on Ganghwa Island. With his blood boiling inside him, Seung Ho clenched his fists tightly as he struggled to control his anger. Seung Jae then enquired the next ferry departure, which turned out to be in the afternoon. The duo was flustered and worried something might happen to Min-hye before they could locate them.

While fretting over the worrisome situation, some fishing boats at the port caught Seung Jae's eyes, he ran over to one of them and pleaded the fishermen to take them to Deokjeokdo Island as they had to attend to an urgent matter, and that he would compensate them with a sum of money. With good luck, one of them agreed to bring them to the island. Once they paid the man and hopped onto the fishing boat, the fisherman started the boat engine and sped off into the vast sea.

On a scenic and tranquil beach of the island, Young-tae and Min-hye were mounding and tamping piles of wet sand to build a sandcastle. However, before they could complete building a sandcastle, the sea water came a rushing and wiped off their unfinished creation. As the weather was getting warmer, Min-hye took off her windbreaker, she laid her jacket on her bag near the edge of the pine tree forest.

After which, she looked around the shore, and picked up a stick to play another game with Young-tae.

She used the stick to draw a line across the sandy beach, and then walked further away from the line. Then she called out for Young-tae to join her position, and explained how the game was to be played.

"Hold the stick upright, bend your body and place your hands and head on the stick, then move your bodies in circles with your head at the centre, when you finished turning, walk to the finishing line over there."

After Min-hye explained the game, she suggested she would play the game first. She took her time and slowly turned her body 5 times around the stick, with Young-tae counting next to her. When she finished turning, she started to walk toward the line, but her body was skewed sideway and moving toward the sea. The swirling effect of the turning had caused Min-hye to walk uncontrollably sideways, she had to consciously pull herself back to walk to the finishing line.

When Min-hye walked like a drunkard and collapsed at the finishing line, Young-tae saw the hilarity of the game and was laughing heartily. In a short while, Min-hye sat on the finishing line and called out to him as it was his turn to play the game. Following Min-hye's cue, he held the stick upright, and circled around the stick 5 times, then the swirling effect took over his brain, and he treaded the sandy beach as slowly as he could so as to stay on course. However, he too almost went into the sea water. His wayward movement was so funny, causing Min-hye to burst into bouts of laughter.

When Young-tae collapsed at the finishing line, he too was laughing at his own silly movements. Then Min-hye suggested circling seven times in the next round. She took her position and turned seven times. With more serious swirling effect in the brain, Min-hye was walking sloppily toward the sea, and was unable to pull herself back to the beach. At first, Young-tae was sitting at the finishing line laughing at her, but he became panic when Min-hye walked waywardly into the sea. He rushed to her and tried to pull her out of the shallow water.

Their clothes were wet, Min-hye was wearing bikinis underneath her blouse, her curvaceous body was visible and sent Young-tae's heart throbbing like raging waves. Her seductive and youthful body had revived all of Young-tae's senses. He felt as though his spirit was being awakened, two decades after Eun-ja passed away. When their eyes met, electrifying currents surged through their bodies and bind them together. As they headed toward the pine tree forest, their lust for each other came full circle, they liberated themselves and made out at the forest.

Alas, the Seung brothers were unable to locate them on time to prevent the affair. After scouring the beaches for half an hour, they finally saw Min-hye's windbreaker lying on the shore, soon they spotted two bodies tangling on the ground at the pine tree forest. They retraced their steps silently and hid behind a rock by the beach.

"It's too late." Whispered Seung Jae to Seung Ho and signalled him to keep quiet. By that time, anger overtook Seung Ho, blood shot up his head and reddened his face, he was shocked by Min-hye's whimsical and flippant conduct. The sight of her tangling with another man amorously had totally blew his mind away, he squatted down on the shore and started weeping. As for Seung Jae, he took out his handphone and captured the copulating scene in a short video, which featured Min-hye's windbreaker in the foreground.

"Let's go before they found out we're here." Seung Jae held Seung Ho's arms to help him stood up. He comforted Seung Ho by putting his arm around Seung Ho's shoulder. They returned to the port of the island looking depressed, especially Seung Ho, he was crestfallen. To avoid taking the same ferry with Min-hye and Young-tae, they looked for the fisherman and paid him for a ride back to Incheon.

Tipping Point

Seung Ho was dispirited since he came back from Deokjeokdo Island, he ignored Min-hye's phone calls, and kept to himself in his room most of the time. Greatly humiliated and angered by Min-hye's betrayal, Seung Ho's heart was aching every second, it seemed to him that a breakup was imminent. Tortured by Min-hye's betrayal, he became emaciated in just a week's time. His parents were worried but Seung Jae did not reveal the details to them. Seung Jae suggested his brother to have an honest talk with Min-hye, but he refused as he did not wish to see Min-hye again. One evening, Seung Jae went to Seung Ho's room before dinner.

"Ho, mom and dad are worried about you, don't behave this way, okay?" Seung Ho was sitting in front of his study table, staring outside the window. It pained Seung Jae to see his brother sank into such a wretched state.

"Jae, I want a breakup, please help me." When he told his brother his decision and asked for his help, it hurt Seung Ho so much that tears fell from his eyes.

"All right, we'll settle this issue together. Let's go for dinner." Seung Jae was glad that his brother had made some sort of a decision, he walked over to him, held his shoulder and patted his back to console him.

On the coming Saturday, Seung Jae called up Min-hye to invite her to his house and talk to Seung Ho. Min-hye agreed instantly as she was not able to reach Seung Ho in the past week. Little did she know that Seung Ho was going to put an end to their relationship. The driver sent her to Seung Ho's house in the afternoon.

"Ho, are you sick? Why didn't you pick up my phone calls?' Min-hye went to Seung Ho's room, saw him sitting in front of his study table. She sat on the edge of Seung Ho's bed, as there was only one chair in the room.

"I'm fine. Where did you go last Saturday? Why didn't you pick up my calls?" As he had decided to break up with Min-hye, Seung Ho was speaking to her in a calm manner.

"I was out picnic with some friends, I forgot to charge my phone battery the night before, my phone battery was flat that day." Min-hye came up with some excuses to hide her affair.

"I remember when you came back from the national park with your tutor, you gave your promise that you would not go out with him again, but you went out with him again last Saturday, right?" Seung Ho confronted her.

"I…how..how did you know? Who told you I went out with him?" Min-hye was taken aback when Seung Ho told her he knew she was with Young-tae last Saturday.

"Don't mind how I get the information, don't be a coward, just admit you went out with him last Saturday." Seung Ho was impatience, he did not intend to tell her he and his brother followed her to the island.

"I…all right…I went out with him last Saturday." Min-hye owned up because she did not like to be called a coward. She had a bad feeling this meeting was heading toward a disaster.

"Tell me where did you go and what did you do with your tutor." Seung Ho demanded to hear the truth from Min-hye herself.

"I…we…were at Deokjeokdo…we're playing games on the beach…that's all…" Min-hye did not have the courage to tell Seung Ho the whole truth.

"Don't lie to me, you made out with him at the pine tree forest, didn't you!" Seung Ho raised his voice when he told her what they did on the island.

"No…no…that's not true…" Seung Ho's knowledge of her affair with Young-tae shocked Min-hye out of her wits and she could not come up with any sensible excuses.

"Was that the first time you made out with him, maybe that was the second time, the first time was at the national park?" Seung Ho grilled Min-hye further like a police interrogator.

"It's not possible to do such a thing at the national park, there are tourists everywhere." Min-hye had to explain nothing happened at the national park, which inadvertently admitted she made out with Young-tae on the island.

"So at Deokjeokdo, it was the first time?" Seung Ho persisted on hearing the truth.

"…that was…yes…" Min-hye finally owned up, "I'm sorry, please forgive me, it won't happen again." She pleaded Seung Ho to forgive her, her eyes began to fill with tears.

"Let's break up, I don't want to see you anymore." After her confession, Seung Ho assertively demanded a breakup.

"No…I don't want to break up with you…please forgive me…I'll not do it again…I promise." Min-hye started crying as she could not accept a breakup and pleaded with Seung Ho to forgive her again.

"Your promise is worthless, I don't trust you anymore, we've to end our relationship today." Seung Ho criticized her behaviour harshly and was adamant on a breakup.

Min-hye had never seen Seung Ho behaving so bitterly cold toward her, there was no way she could salvage their relationship with his determination. She left Seung Ho's house in distraught as she did not expect Seung Ho to find out her affairs with her tutor and end up put an end to their relationship.

Seung Jae entered Seung Ho's room as soon as Min-hye left the house, he saw Seung Ho was still sitting in front of his study table, but his face was covered with tears.

"It's okay now, don't be sad anymore." A concerned Seung Jae hugged his brother and comforted him.

"Jae, I hope the recording goes well, let's check." Seung Ho wiped off his tears and lifted a piece of paper on his table, where a small voice recorder was placed underneath. They played the voice recorder and found Min-hye's confession had been recorded clearly.

"Jae, we now have the short video clip and voice recording, what if Min-hye's dad beat her up when he found out her affair with the tutor?" Seung Ho was worried the revelation to Mr Choi would cause problem for Min-hye.

"I'll try to appeal to Mr Choi not to hurt Min-hye, after all, she's a victim like other girls." Seung Jae made a call to the Choi mansion, introduced who he was, and spoke with Mr Choi briefly and arranged a meeting with him to discuss an important matter.

It was a peaceful and quiet evening at a country club restaurant where Seung Jae and Seung Ho were supposed to meet Mr Choi.

"Uncle Choi." Seung Ho saw Mr Choi entered the restaurant and called out for him. The brothers stood up and waited for Mr Choi to be seated.

"Seung Ho, is this your brother whom I spoke to over the phone yesterday?" Mr Choi asked Seung Ho, he was unaware of the matter they were about to reveal to him.

"Yes, this is Seung Jae, my eldest brother." Seung Ho introduced his brother to Mr Choi.

"Good evening, uncle Choi." Seung Jae greeted Mr Choi and bowed slightly.

"All right, what's the important matter that you wish to discuss with me?" Mr Choi ordered a cup of tea before they started their conversation.

"Uncle Choi, you know Min-hye's tutor, Mr Joo Young-tae?" Seung Jae mentioned Young-tae's name to start off their conversation.

"Yes, Young-tae is a competent tutor and an outstanding banker, what about him?" Mr Choi told them his impression of Young-tae.

"Please view this short video clip." Seung Jae showed Mr Choi the video clip on his handphone.

Mr Choi took his handphone and viewed the video clip carefully. He put down the phone when the video clip ended.

"This windbreaker looks familiar, I've seen it somewhere." Mr Choi was trying to recall the owner of the windbreaker, he did not see the two people at the pine tree forest.

"Uncle Choi, this windbreaker belongs to Min-hye. Look at the two persons in the forest, they are Min-hye and her tutor." Seung Jae played the video clip again and pointed out to Mr Choi the two people lying on the ground of the forest.

"What? How could this happen? Are you sure that is Min-hye? I can't see her face at all." Mr Choi was doubtful and could not believe Min-hye would be intimately involved with her tutor.

"Yes, uncle Choi, they made out at the forest on Deokjeokdo the Saturday before last. Please don't be angry with Min-hye, she is a victim. This tutor had engaged in illicit affairs with other girls before."

Seung Jae took out the voice recorder and Min-hye's confession was played.

"I'm sure you recognize Min-hye's voice. Please don't get too upset. We wish you could make a decision, that is to prevent the tutor from preying on other victims by making a police report." It was out of respect to inform Min-hye's father about the affairs.

"This is infuriating! Scumbag! Low-life!" Mr Choi's temper flared, he was fuming mad as he cursed at Young-tae's illicit behaviour with his daughter.

"Uncle Choi, I've been to Ganghwado and learned that he had an intimate affair with a local girl. I don't know whether there are other victims." Seung Jae told Mr Choi, hopefully Mr Choi would make a police report with these evidence.

"Thank you, I'm really upset about this, let me go back and consider. Can you send me the video clip and voice recording within the next few days?" Outraged and confused by the revelation, Mr Choi was not ready to make a decision on the spot.

"Yes, uncle Choi, please understand, I'll only send them to you when you decide to make a police report." Implored Seung Jae, he contemplated to report to the police if Mr Choi did not take action.

"All right, I've to listen to what Min-hye has to say about this." Explained Mr Choi, he thanked the brothers and hurriedly left the restaurant.

On this Sunday morning, Young-tae, dressed in a black and white three-piece suit, was waiting at his apartment for the groomsman to fetch him to the outdoor wedding venue. Whereas, as he opened the door after hearing the door bell, several men entered his apartment, they showed him their police batches, and arrested him under the charges of engaging in under-aged sex. He was put on handcuffs and brought to the police station.

Rui-a was in her wedding gown getting ready for their wedding ceremony, some of the guests had arrived and the venue was filled with blissful music and pleasant chatters. While she was taking pictures with some relatives, she received a call from the groomsman saying Young-tae had been arrested and was now at the police station. Upon hearing Young-tae was charged with engaging in illicit activities with minors, Rui-a suffered a blackout and fainted.

Chp 9

◆

Inmate 31847

Young-tae was charged in court for engaging under-aged sex with three minors aged between 15 and 16, he was sentenced to five and a half years in jail. He pleaded guilty before the commencement of the court hearings so that the victims did not have to appear in court as witnesses, which was to protect them from the public eyes.

The day had arrived for Young-tae to begin his imprisonment at Pohang prison. A set of prison uniform was given to him to change into before he was directed to his cell. The prison shirt was printed with the numbers 31847. He was also instructed to remove any accessories on his body.

"You can't take this away…I'm keeping this…" There was a squabble between Young-tae and one of the prison wardens who was instructing him to surrender the silver chain and ring he had on his neck.

"Nobody is allowed to wear accessories in the prison, hand it over to me right now." The straight faced warden gave a stern command as he extended his hand in front of

Young-tae, prompting him to place the silver chain and ring on his palm.

"No! I have to keep this with me! Please let me keep it!" Young-tae shielded the silver chain and ring with both hands on his chest and refused to barge.

"31847, how dare you create trouble on your first day in prison?! You should bear in mind who is in charge here!" The warden then signalled to two officers nearby. The two officers came over to Young-tae, one of them grabbed his left arm and the other grabbed his right, and they bent his arms behind his back. Young-tae struggled vehemently to break off the restraints, but his struggle was futile.

"31847, you must obey the rules here starting this minute!" In a fit of anger, the warden pulled off the silver chain from his neck using brute force.

"Bring him to his cell." The warden then told the two officers who were holding Young-tae's hands tightly behind his back, and they clutched him all the way to his cell.

Locked in his cell, he had his fingers firmly clenched on the grilled door, he pleaded to the officers to return the ring to him, but they left the cell heedless of his plea. Since Eun-ja's death, he had never taken the silver ring off his neck. The ring symbolized the spirit of Eun-ja, losing it was tantamount to losing Eun-ja, he could not lose her once again. The fear of losing the ring engulfed his soul, his face looked confused and tormented.

The affliction had caused panic and anxiety in him, he soon spiralled into a series of erratic behaviour. He was kicking the iron grilled door, hoping an officer would hear him, when nobody paid attention to him, he gave up and crouched his body in a corner. Burying his face in his hands, he was weeping and mumbling he had let Eun-ja down once again. After a while, he stood up and leaned on the wall, knocking his head and banging his fists on the concrete surface.

He would then go back to the door, clenched his fingers on the iron grill again, and repeatedly raising his voice asking the officers to return the ring to him. He kept these routines several times until he was exhausted and curled himself up in a corner.

It was 7 o'clock in the evening, the inmates were released and moved to the dining hall for dinner. After queuing up for the food and drinks, the inmates would find a place to sit down and eat their dinner. Looking dispirited and annoyed, Young-tae sat in front of his dinner, he drank some water, but did not eat a morsel, while the other inmates were tucking down their food.

One warden noticed that Young-tae did not touch his food, he came over to instruct him to hurry up and finish his dinner.

"I'm not eating, I don't have appetite." Said Young-tae when the warden asked him to eat his dinner.

"Eat up or else you'll be hungry later. You must obey the rules here." The warden reminded him to abide by the prison rules and regulations.

"Give back my ring!" Young-tae suddenly raised his voice and stared at the warden fiercely. He then stood up, lifted the tray and hurled it off the table to release his pent up anger. The food and tray flew in the air, and landed on the ground with a loud clang, some rice, vegetable and meat were scattered on the floor.

The clunking noise immediately put all the officers in the hall on their guards, to prevent a mess riot, they swiftly surrounded the inmates table by table with their batons in their hands. The hall became quiet all of a sudden. All eyes were on Young-tae, he had his arms clutched behind his back almost instantly by two officers. One of the senior wardens came over to his table.

"31847, there'll be no dinner for you for three days. If you throw tantrums again, you'll be locked up in solitary confinement immediately!" The senior warden then told the two officers to bring him back to his cell.

The first day in the prison was nightmarish for Young-tae, in the afternoon, he was defiant and his temper flared in front of everybody, at night he endured hunger pangs for hours until he fell asleep. In the middle of the night, he dreamt about his silver ring.

In his dream, he was looking for his silver ring in a forest, he lost his way in the vast forest and was wandering aimlessly. Finally, a tiny sparkle on a tree caught his eyes, he quickly ran towards the direction of the shining object, and to his delight, it was exactly the silver ring he was looking for. He was thrilled as he took the silver ring from the tree and put the chain on his neck. In a split second, the tree transformed into a faceless spirit. The spirit donned a long black robe, it raised the dagger in its hand and stabbed into Young-tae's chest. His dream ended here as he woke up crying "No!", with his heart pounding and his body broke into cold sweats.

Having had his silver ring taken away, Young-tae was behaving as if his spirit had vanished, he looked like a deflated balloon, dragging himself through the daily routines without any vitality. His eyes were avoiding contacts, his mouth tightly shut, and his demeanour gloomy.

One afternoon, an unexpected visitor, Dr Kang Woo-hyun, his psychiatrist, came to visit him.

"It's good to see you, Young-tae." Dr Kang initiated the greeting when Young-tae sat down at the other side of the glass panel.

"How are you Dr Kang? Why are you here?" Young-tae exchanged the greetings, looking languorous and unenthusiastic.

"See what I've got here." Dr Kang took out Young-tae's silver chain and ring from an envelope.

"It's my ring!" Proclaimed Young-tae, it was a pleasant surprise to him. He stood up and leaned forward to take a closer look.

"Yes, it's your ring." Smiled Dr Kang as he saw some reaction from Young-tae.

"Are you returning it to me now?" Asked Young-tae eagerly, his face lit up in an instant.

"No, you can't wear any accessories in the prison. The authority has instructed me to pass this ring to Rui-a. Can you trust Rui-a to keep this for you until you are released?" Dr Kang was entrusted with a mission.

"I guess so." Disappointed with Dr Kang's reply, Young-tae said in a dissatisfied tone as he sat down.

"Dr Kang, when you see Rui-a, tell her not to visit me, I'm too ashamed to face her." Young-tae requested a favour from Dr Kang.

"I'll pass the message to her." Replied Dr Kang. "There's another matter I wish to discuss with you."

"What is it?" Asked Young-tae flatly, looking uninterested.

"I'm also instructed to assess your condition and prescribe a medication for you, maybe for a course of one year or two." Dr Kang revealed his second mission.

"I don't need any medication." Said Young-tae tersely, as he was annoyed by the idea.

"Don't worry, it's not a serious matter. I guess you've not been eating sufficiently, the authority was concerned, so I was summoned here to give an assessment on your health condition." Explained Dr Kang.

"Do I look sickly to you? You're a psychiatrist, can you prescribe non-psychiatric medications?" Young-tae was puzzled with Dr Kang's professional practice.

"Well, I used to be a medical doctor in a hospital before I became a psychiatrist, so I'm certified to prescribe non-psychiatric medication as well. You look rather emaciated, it's better to have some treatment before your condition gets worse. Starting tomorrow, the wardens will give you the medication during meal times." Replied Dr Kang as he analysed Young-tae's physical appearance.

"It's time for me to leave, I'll see you next month for another assessment. Take care." Dr Kang bade his goodbye and left the meeting room.

The next month Dr Kang visited Young-tae again for another assessment and delivered another course of medication. That day, Mdm Shim came to visit as well, she met Young-tae after Dr Kang finished his session.

"Auntie, I'm sorry." Young-tae felt tremendous guilt when he saw Mdm Shim, the first thing came to his mind was to apologize.

"Young-tae, we're worried about you. You've lost weight. Why won't you let Rui-a visit you?" Mdm Shim expressed her concern.

"I'm too ashamed of myself for betraying her love and loyalty to me. Auntie, no matter what I say or do I can't redeem my sin." Young-tae told Mdm Shim why he could not face Rui-a.

"Rui-a was miserable when Dr Kang told her you don't want to see her." Mdm Shim tried to change Young-tae's mind to let Rui-a visit him.

"I just can't face her, Auntie, please tell her I'm truly sorry about my mistakes, and that I could never be able to provide her a normal and happy life." Young-tae thought it would be better for Rui-a to move on and get married to someone else.

"You know she's always busy, can you see her when she's free?" Mdm Shim asked again, ignoring his declaration.

"Auntie…" Young-tae was at a loss for words, Mdm Shim seemed so persistent on this issue.

"Young-tae, we've known each other for decades, do you think we can just ignore your existence? We would be condemned if we cut off our ties with you when you're in trouble. We're miserable as well, but we're your family, we'll face the tough time together and overcome the obstacle together." Mdm Shim reminded him of their long-standing relationship and that they should share weal and woe in life.

Young-tae was deeply touched by Mdm Shim's sincerity, he realized he had a responsibility in this family. Even when he was in the most disgraceful and desolate situation, he could not neglect their feelings and their existence. Nevertheless, he thought, he had done irreversible damage to their relationship, and there was no turning back.

"Auntie, I'm a sinner, I'm no longer worthy of your love and concern. Don't visit me again, and don't forgive me as I've betrayed and destroyed our kinship. I should disappear in your lives so that all of you can live in peace. As for Rui-a, I don't deserve her love anymore, she should meet someone compatible and live a happy and blissful life." Reiterated Young-tae of his decision to sever their ties.

"We're your family, I treat you like a son, you can't treat us like strangers…I know you're suffering, you may be giving up on yourself, but you can't give up our relationship. I'll leave now, Rui-a will visit you soon when she's free." Mdm Shim felt miserable as she could tell that Young-tae's spirit was completely crushed, he was not the Young-tae they used to know.

Mdm Shim was slightly worked up as she could not change Young-tae's mind. She left the meeting room without waiting for his reply.

A Bundle of Joy

A few months after Young-tae went to jail, Rui-a gave birth to a baby boy in the hospital. Mr Jang, Rui-a's father, came to visit her and the new born baby. Mr Jang was a carpenter, he owned a furniture shop in the suburban area where Rui-a was brought up. The birth of his grandson was a blissful event and had brought ineffable joy to him. Beneath the cloudy atmosphere, although Young-tae, the father of the baby, was locked up in prison, a rejoicing mood prevailed as they welcomed the little new member to their family.

Mdm Shim was busy as she had to take care of her grandson as well as Rui-a's confinement diet. Although much work had to be done for the baby, they were basking in the blissfulness of the addition of a new family member. All their focus and attention were on the baby. Even Joo-a was really fond of her nephew, the first thing she came back from school was to hold the baby, tickle him on the chin, help to change his diapers, and feed him milk.

Mr Jang visited them more often over the weekends. One day, they were chatting over dinner.

"Mom, dad, should we tell Young-tae about the baby? I wonder how he would react." Rui-a asked her parents whether to tell Young-tae about the baby.

"The last time I visited him he looked absolutely despondent, I don't think it's the right time to tell him, he might feel more pressurized since he could not do anything for the baby and you." Mdm Shim deliberated the situation.

"I agree, it's better not to confuse him further, since he's under a lot of stress right now. Imagine he knows he has a son, but he could not see him or take care of him, how would he feel? He would feel guilty as he can't fulfil the responsibility of a father. Let the imprisonment slowly dissolves his tribulation, thereafter, he should take on the new responsibility." Mr Jang voiced his concern and opinion as he supported his wife's point of view.

"Dad, I wonder if he still have any feelings for me." Rui-a was worried Young-tae would never see her again.

"He's likely to be pessimistic and unenthusiastic at the moment, let's just exercise some patience for the time being." Said Mr Jang, he thought it was inappropriate to dwell into such an issue at that time.

"Rui-a, when you visit him, talk about daily stuff, don't talk about anything sensitive. Ahh....Young-tae has been suffering silently for years after Eun-ja passed away suddenly, he's really pitiful." Although Young-tae's erroneous behaviour had caused damage to their relationship, Mdm Shim was sympathetic of his plight.

"I remember Eun-ja's death has traumatized Young-tae to the extent that he could not focus on his studies and didn't to go to school for a long time. Fortunately, he resumed schooling the next year, and all he did was to spend most of his time studying and helping his parents in the farm when he's free. Ahh...we're all subject to the vicissitude of life, but his life is destined to be tougher than a lot of us." Lamented Mr Jang, of the tough situation Young-tae was facing.

Her Forgiveness was Unbearable

It was one month after Rui-a had given birth to her baby boy when she first visited Young-tae in prison.

"Young-tae, how are you?" Rui-a was concerned as Young-tae looked rather haggard and spiritless.

"Your mom didn't tell you not to visit me?" Young-tae seemed annoyed as he tried to put his message across.

"I know you're ashamed of yourself, you feel guilty when you see us, but we've known each other for years, do you think we can just ignore you and leave you alone and let you suffer by yourself? I'm miserable, because I was at fault too, since I started working as an architect, I was too busy and neglected you, I wasn't sensitive enough toward your feelings and needs, I'm truly sorry." Rui-a could not bear to let Young-tae shoulder all the suffering, she confessed that she was at fault too.

"How can it be your fault? I've done irreversible damage to our relationship, nothing I do or say will revert to the amicable relationship we used to have, please leave and don't visit me again." Young-tae seemed to be adamant about his decision.

"No! That's selfish of you, you only think about your own suffering, you've to spare a thought for me as well, my feelings for you is deep, it's genuine, we're like a family, there's no doubt about it. I'm sure you have feelings for me, my mom, dad, and Joo-a, you can't write off our relationship just like that." Argued Rui-a, for she could not imagine a life without Young-tae, especially when they have a son now.

"My head is so heavy, it's about to explode. Don't try to rationalize things or sympathize with me, it's useless. I need to be left alone, I'm truly sorry for causing so much pain and discomfort in your lives." Young-tae was suffering from a headache as he talked to Rui-a. His wretched look had begun to sadden Rui-a.

"My dear, my heart aches when you say that, I know it's hard for you to spare a thought for my feelings right now, but I need to let you know that I've forgiven you and I'll always love you." Rui-a could not fight back her tears anymore, she was tormented as she could not persuade Young-tae into accepting her love again. He seemed to have completely shut himself out from the world.

"Ahh, don't…don't…forgive me, I don't deserve your forgiveness. You should reprimand me, abuse me, throw things at me, humiliate me, and vent all your anger on me, but please don't…don't….love me anymore." It was too late for regrets, thought Young-tae, as tears flew down his face. He would rather Rui-a take it out on him, as her forgiveness was unbearably heavy for his shrivelled psyche. The fact that he had betrayed the persons who had known him, trusted him and loved him for two decades had caused tremendous regrets in him, and that he should be condemned and should not be forgiven.

"I'm sorry, but I can't agree with what you've said. I'll visit you again next month, meanwhile, please take care of yourself." Said Rui-a as she dried her tears, and left the meeting room.

Before Rui-a paid another visit to the prison, she put up a request to the authority to allow Young-tae to paint pictures in prison. She had been exploring the possibility for Young-tae's paintings to be sold to property developers and hoteliers. When she was free over the weekends, she would also take a trip to one of the islands to take photos of different landscapes for Young-tae's painting guide.

"Young-tae, I'm glad you're looking better today." Rui-a put up a smile when she saw Young-tae for the second time in prison.

"How's everybody at home?" There was a change in Young-tae's attitude from the last visit, he was sitting upright and talking to Rui-a in a friendly composure.

"Everybody is fine. The authority has agreed to allow you to paint, I've brought your painting stuff, the wardens will pass them to you later." Rui-a was glad that it was easier for her to communication with him this time round.

"That's really helpful, it would be a good pastime as I'm rather bored in here." Young-tae welcomed the pleasant surprise.

"It should be more than a pastime, I've talked to some hoteliers and property developers, they are interested if your paintings are suitable for the interior decoration of their buildings. Let me know if you need anything beside the stuff I sent you, I'll get them for you. I've also taken some landscape pictures for you to base your paintings on." Explained Rui-a, Young-tae was encouraged to take the painting more seriously.

"As long as you paint the way you did before, I guess it should be fine." Rui-a went on saying.

"Hopefully I can still paint good pictures, I'm really thankful to you for going through the trouble so that I can start painting again." Young-tae expressed his appreciation.

"I've confidence you could do a good job." Rui-a maintained her optimism towards Young-tae's painting skills.

"My erroneous behaviour must have caused tremendous heartache for you, right?" Young-tae was hoping his mistakes did not cause too much suffering to Rui-a.

"Hmm… On our wedding ceremony, I passed out when I received the call saying you were arrested and sent to the police station. As soon as I regained consciousness, I had a change of clothes and rushed to the police station to find out the truth. Before I could speak to you, I saw Mr Choi cursing and throwing files and stationery at you. I hid behind a wall for fear you would be embarrassed if you see me. My heart was broken into pieces when you did not defend yourself, as I know you must have committed the felony, otherwise, you would have denied it. I covered my mouth and cried silently, it was a really tough day for me. That night, I locked myself in the room and got drunk to avoid answering mom's questions. I went through the next day in a daze, I could not visit you as I was too distraught, I was lying in bed most of the time, feeling depressed and blaming myself for not spending enough time with you." Rui-a gave an account of her experience on the day she received the news of Young-tae's arrest.

"It's entirely my fault, nobody else is at fault. I'm truly sorry." It saddened Young-tae when Rui-a told him she passed out and was devastated over his arrest.

"Tell me how you meet Kim Suk-mi. There should be no secret between us, please tell me what happened, I promise I won't ask you again." Rui-a decided to learn the details of the affairs and hoped that Young-tae could be honest about them.

"I met her on Gangwado, she is an inhabitant on that island. That day she had a tiff with her boyfriend, she went to the mountain to take her mind off the squabble. We sat on a small patch of empty ground near the trail and chatted for a while. She confided in me with the problems she had and we became friends since that day. I went to the island several times, we met again and made out near the area. I guess we found solace in each other's company." Young-tae confessed to Rui-a on his intimate encounters with Kim Suk-mi.

Rui-a was disgusted with the account of the affairs, she suddenly felt there was a lack of oxygen in her brain, which caused her to feel dizzy momentarily.

"How many times did you make out with her?" Although she felt a strong sense of contempt to their affairs, and despised the persons who had betrayed their relationships, she had decided to get a full picture of all his affairs.

"Twice, at the same place. Remember someone attacked me from behind on Ganghwado, and I had to wear a neck cast? Her boyfriend did that to me when he found out our affairs." Young-tae recalled the time when he was brutally attacked from behind on the island.

Rui-a was feeling nauseated as Young-tae, the person whom she had trusted and loved for so many years, talked about his intimate affairs with girls. Her tolerance had diminished somewhat, she could not fathom how they could be so frivolous and irresponsible.

"What about Choi Min-hye, your tuition student?" Asked Rui-a, as she tried real hard to have her tumultuous emotions under-wrapped.

"You sure you want to hear this, you look rather uncomfortable." Asked Young-tae as he noticed Rui-a was going through some mental struggle by the look of her slightly irritated expression.

"Don't mind me, tell me everything once and for all, and I won't ask you again in future." Insisted Rui-a, as she took a deep breath to gain some mental strength for the next revelation.

"Min-hye was in good spirit after she gained remarkable improvement in her tests, she wanted to go on an island trip with me. I brought her to Deokjeokdo one Saturday. We were playing a really fun game by the beach, we're laughing uncontrollably and really had a great time. I got panic when she fell into the sea, so I rushed over to pull her out of the water. We got carried away and made out at the pine tree forest. I wasn't thinking, everything happened real quick that day." Young-tae recalled the affair with Min-hye on Deokjeokdo Island.

"How many times did you do it with this rich kid?" Rui-a was getting upset with the revelation.

"Once, someone took a short video clip with his handphone, and reported our affair to her father. Her father blew his top and made a police report." Young-tae told Rui-a how his affair with Min-hye was discovered.

Rui-a felt sick in the stomach, her mouth was dry and her mind disturbed. She summoned all her strength to expel her disgust and contempt so as to endure one last confession.

"What happened when you and Joo-a went to the park? All I know was she fell down a slope." Rui-a was dreary that she would suffer a nervous breakdown after listening to the intimate affair between Young-tae and her younger sister.

"It's hard for you to hear this, let's skip this incident." Suggested Young-tae as he too was afraid Rui-a might suffer a breakdown.

"No! Tell me once and for all, I don't freaking care if I passed out again!" Rui-a was furious, the language was crude. That was the first time she used harsh words on Young-tae in their decade long relationship.

"All right, I'm truly sorry. That day Joo-a fell and tumbled down a slope, she was lying at the bottom of the slope, moaning. I was so terrified, Eun-ja's accident flashed across my mind and I thought Joo-a was going to die. The fear of losing her was overwhelming, I couldn't help but to hold her and massage her back and arms, I couldn't let go of her. She was holding me tightly, soon we lost ourselves in the alluring chemistry, and made out at the bottom of the slope." Young-tae felt a sense of relief as he had done disclosing his affairs with the girls, however, by now, Rui-a felt regretful that the normalcy of her life had been befouled by his infidelity and criminal behaviours.

The end of the revelation had cast Rui-a into a dark and gloomy psyche. She sat silently trying to get a hold of herself. Again, she summoned all her mental strength to suppress her deepest abhorrence toward these affairs without uttering a single word. Then she stood up abruptly and left the visiting room without bidding goodbye to Young-tae.

When she got into her car, she let go of her pent-up emotions and cried her heart out. That night, she returned home feeling miserable, and got herself drunk in her room, for the second time in her life.

Chp 10

◆

Journey to Freedom

It takes about five hours to drive from Pohang province to Seoul remand centre. When the languished looking Young-tae stepped out of the prison gate, he saw a police officer standing next to a dark blue coloured police vehicle and signalling at him to board the car.

"I'm Officer Park. Your journey will be officially ended once we reached the Seoul remand centre. When you are out of the gate of the remand centre, never look back." Said the officer without turning his head as Young-tae settled down in the rear seat.

"Yes, Sir." Replied Young-tae quietly.

The stigma of an imprisonment record had occupied his mind since he stepped out of the prison gate, he realised that it would stay with him forever. This harrowing thought had further cast a shadow on his languished stature.

He had been staring at the scenery outside the window since the vehicle was in motion. After about half an hour into the journey without any conversation, Officer Park broke the silence, "Last week a ferry bound for Jeju Island capsized near Jindo Island, have you heard of this news?"

The news caught Young-tae's attention, so he looked in front and switched his focus on the conversation.

"No, I don't know about this news. How many people were on board? Anybody hurt?" Replied Young-tae.

"It's a darn disaster! More than 400 people were on board the ferry and only 174 people survived! There are still a lot of passengers missing. Most of them are high school students from Ansan city, they were going for a field trip on Jeju Island." Officer Park recounted the numbers involved in the disaster with indignation, which resonated the sentiment of many Koreans who were affected emotionally by the accident.

"Oh dear, what a tragedy! The victims' parents must be totally heart-broken!" Young-tae heaved a heavy sigh and listened on. Officer Park continued to fill him in with the details and occasionally aired his personal opinion.

"Ahh...my stomach is rumbling! I'm famished! We are now at Jung-gu of Daejeon city, we'll take a break here." As the car came to a stop in front of a small Korean eatery, Officer Park handed over a paper bag to Young-tae.

"What's inside this bag? Who gave it to me?" Young-tae did not expect such a gesture.

"There is a shirt in the bag, a pair of pants, socks, shoes, underwear, and a piece of hankerchief. A friend of yours put up a formal request to the authority to have this handed to you when you are out..." Officer Park carefully omitted the word 'prison'.

Young-tae thought to himself, who else but Rui-A would do this for him.

"We'll take a break for lunch at this eatery. Change into the new clothes in the washroom and throw away what you are wearing, it's a symbolic gesture of leaving the unpleasant past behind." Officer Park said in a serious tone for fear that Young-tae would not comply.

Officer Park got out of the vehicle and headed toward the eatery, Young-tae carried the paper bag and followed him. They were promptly greeted as they entered the eatery. Officer Park returned the greetings, found a table and sat down, while Young-tae asked for the washroom's direction.

"What kind of food do you wish to have?" A middle-aged woman came over to take order from Officer Park. "Please give us two bowls of kimchi ramen with pork, a bowl of soup with square tofu, and two cups of coffee." Officer Park ordered tofu for Young-tae as it is a common practise in South Korea for a person to eat tofu when he just got out of prison. He ordered simple lunch so they could return to Seoul without much delay.

After changing into the new clothes, Young-tae put all the old clothes in the paper bag and washed his face at the toilet's basin. As he took out the hankerchief from his pants' side pocket to wipe his face, he noticed there was something wrapped in it, he unwrapped it and found a stack of 50,000 won banknotes.

Rui-a must have given them to him, he thought. But instead of being touched by the thoughtful gesture, his heart was heavy with guilt as he had betrayed her and damaged their relationship. All the while when he was in the prison, he could not think of a way to make it up to her, and thought the best for both of them was that she had already gotten married.

Looking into the mirror, Young-tae felt a bit light hearted with the new image. Washing his face had lifted his spirit somewhat. He came out of the washroom looking fresh, spotted Officer Park and joined him at the dining table. "I need to go to the washroom, please take your meal, I'll join you later." Officer Park took out his mobile phone as he walked toward the washroom.

At this time, the food was served and Young-tae settled the bill right away with the money in his pocket. They returned to the vehicle after lunch. Before they boarded the vehicle again, Officer Park glanced at the paper bag in Young-tae's hand, Young-tae took the hint and dumped it in a garbage bin outside the eatery.

After another hour on the road, they finally reached the remand centre. The vehicle came to a stop at the car park, they got out of the car and shook hands with each other.

"Thank you for sending me back." Young-tae bowed slightly to show his appreciation. Officer Park patted him on his back and reminded him, "Take care, walk straight to the main road and don't turn your head back!"

"Yes, sir." Young-tae replied. Ingeniously, that was exactly the same two words he uttered when he first met Officer Park that morning.

Stepping into the Real World

Young-tae began his journey to total freedom, suppressing the urge to look back and wave goodbye to Officer

Park, he managed to walk pass the gate and head toward the main road looking straight ahead.

As he came to the main road, he felt a sudden surge of sadness in his heart. Tears filled his eyes as he was overwhelmed by the long awaited freedom. Wiping off his tears, he took a deep breath and walked on.

He had made up his mind to sell his apartment and go back to his hometown to join his parents and earn a living as a farmer. The outlook of a simple and secluded life was rather comforting to his tattered soul at that moment.

While he was trudging by the side of the main road, he heard a familiar voice calling out to him.

"Young-tae! Young-tae!" Mdm Shim stuck her head out of the front seat window of a white sedan, smiling and waving at Young-tae. Just when Young-tae turned his head to the direction of the voice, he saw Rui-a stepping out of the car.

Even though deep down he felt like running away, he had to face them with all the shame and guilt in his soul, after all, they were the ones whom he shared precious moments with in the past twenty over years. On the other hand, he thought these two magnanimous souls must be angels in disguise, warming the hearts of the distressed and giving them tremendous inner strength. He also knew that these two familiar faces would bring up memories and stir up emotions, so he reminded himself to mind his words and check his behaviours.

Casting aside the awkwardness in the atmosphere, Rui-a smiled slightly and said, "Let's go home." Then she walked over and ushered him to the rear seat of the car.

"Auntie Shim, how have you been?" Young-tae greeted Mdm Shim politely once he entered the car.

"Oh, I have been busy looking after the household. Fortunately my health does not give me a lot of trouble, it is just that my cholesterol and blood pressure are a bit high, that's all. You look healthy, that is really a great relief to me." Said Mdm Shim warmly to foster a relax atmosphere.

"Mom's blood pressure rose since Joo-a went to study in Australia, is that right, mom?" Asked Rui-a while maneuvering the steering wheel.

"Last year, before Joo-a went to Australia, she was very reluctant to study abroad. She said she couldn't bear to leave all of us behind, but when she was there, within half a year, she found herself a boyfriend! What a wilful girl she is! I was worried she would neglect her studies so I scolded her. She threatened if I kept scolding her she would stay in Australia and never come back! I'm at my wits' end, she thinks she is a grown-up now and wants to live her life according to her own will. What can I do?" Mdm Shim lamented.

"At least her boyfriend can look after her while she's in Australia, don't worry, I'll keep an eye on her." Said Rui-a, trying to pacify her mother.

"You are too optimistic and too lenient with her, we can't monitor her from South Korea!" Mdm Shim chided Rui-a.

"Mom, I told her she has to perform well in her studies, or else I'll cut her pocket money, then she would have to take up a part time job to pay for her daily expenses." Rui-a replied with confidence.

After hearing that Joo-a was now studying in Australia, Young-tae breathed a quiet sigh of relief as he would feel ashamed if he saw Joo-a again. Returning to the world of people who had loved and trusted him before was by no means an easy thing to do.

"Auntie, I'm truly sorry for causing hurt to Joo-a, and betrayed the love you and Rui-a had given me. I'm sorry from the bottom of my heart." Said Young-tae remorsefully.

"I know you are truly sorry about the past, your life is not easy since you lost Eun-ja at the tender age of 16. Now that heaven has taken away five years of your precious life, you have been punished for your wrongdoings. Hopefully, we can all leave the unpleasant past behind and be responsible for our future endeavours from now on." Mdm Shim's amiable attitude toward Young-tae had caused some resentment from Rui-a.

"My dear mom, if you could treat Joo-a like you treat Young-tae today, I think she won't disobey you all the time. That's really patriarchal!" Protested Rui-a.

"What a mean daughter you are, dare to criticise your own mother!" Chided Mdm Shim. Her futile complaint had caused a silent chuckle in both Young-tae and Rui-a.

Then Young-tae could not help but asked Rui-a, "Whose house are you taking me?"

"It's your house, we are going to your house, but before that we have to go pick up someone on the way." Rui-a replied with a smile.

"But this is not the way to my apartment..." Asked Young-tae.

"I'm sorry, I should have told you earlier that I have used some of your money to buy a new house. Your previous apartment has been sold." Replied Rui-a.

"How did you sell it without my consent?" Young-tae was rather perplexed when he heard that.

"I acted as your guardian and made the decision, I'm sorry." Said Rui-a, then she cast a quick glance at Mdm Shim. Mdm Shim then pressed a button on the vehicle's audio system, and some music of children songs streamed from the stereo.

Young-tae could not continue with his queries as he was interrupted by the music. Then it dawned on him that Rui-a had gotten married and was now a mother.

"So you have a child?" Asked Young-tae, while the melodious and joyful children songs filled the atmosphere.

"Yes. We have to go pick him up now." Replied Rui-a briefly as she pulled up the vehicle in front of a childcare centre. "Mom, please go and fetch little Taek, we will wait in the car." Said Rui-a to Mdm Shim.

A short while later, Mdm Shim returned with her grandson. She opened the rear door of the sedan and helped little Taek climbed onto the rear seat.

"Little Taek, are you comfortable sitting at the back?" Asked Rui-a.

"Yes, mommy." Replied little Taek as he scrutinized Young-tae with his little inquisitive eyes.

"Good afternoon." Young-tae said hello first. It had been ages since he came into contact with small children. Young-tae thought he should at least put up a smile, so as not to frighten him.

"Good afternoon. My name is little Taek, may I know what is your name?" Little Taek asked.

"My name is Joo Young-tae, nice to meet you." Replied Young-tae.

Upon hearing the name 'Joo Young-tae', little Taek asked, "Do you know that I'm your son?"

Young-tae was taken aback with this question, so dumb founded that he could only shake his head in slow motions. "Rui-a, can you...?" Young-tae was totally baffled and asked for help.

However much Rui-a had mentally prepared for this moment, she could not offer any verbal help to Young-tae at that juncture. An emotional confession was imminent. She drove to a small car park next to some provision shops and stopped the car there.

"Mom, can you bring little Taek to the shop for some ice-cream while I talk to Young-tae?" Requested Rui-a.

"Okay." Said Mdm Shim, then she carried her grandson from the rear seat and went to a grocery shop nearby.

"Let's talk outside. I'm feeling rather stuffy in here." Said Rui-a. They got out of the car and went to a corner of the open car park.

"If you are thinking of finding a surrogate father for your son, you are looking at the wrong person!" Said Young-tae vehemently. "Are you out of your mind? I've a criminal record, I'm not fit to be anybody's father!"

"Calm down, please listen to me. I'm sorry, I'm really sorry. I know it's my fault, I should have told you earlier about little Taek, please forgive me." Rui-a began her ardent quest for forgiveness.

"I was pregnant at the beginning of your jail term. Remember your company opened a new branch and you were promoted as the manager? We were so happy and went to celebrate at a jazz bar? After that you spent a night at my house and we made out in my bedroom. I found out I was pregnant one week after you were in jail. I was frightened and confused, and could not tell anyone until mom noticed my stomach was beginning to swell." Rui-a was intimidated as Young-tae was staring hard at her, her eyes were brimming with tears.

"Tell me he's not my son! I can't be anybody's father!" Young-tae exclaimed in denial and started to grab Rui-a's arms. As he shook her bodies back and forth, he felt as though all the blood in his body had rushed into his head. He then let go of her arms, sat on a kerb, and buried his face in his hands.

"Little Taek is 4 years old, he is really your son. You should know you are the only man in my life. You can bring little Taek to the hospital for a DNA examination tomorrow if you need assurance." Rui-a began sobbing as she was affected by Young-tae's harsh reaction.

"Stop crying! Tell me why you keep me in the dark about little Taek, after so many years! You even sold my apartment without telling me. What a wicked woman you are!" Young-tae could not accept that Rui-a had kept mum with these events. Though still in shock, Young-tae demanded an explanation while trying to calm down.

"If you know I was pregnant, you would ask me to have an abortion! I didn't want to hear that from you! Even mom didn't force me to abort the child, she could accept the reality, why can't you? Moreover, I was in my thirties and I really wanted to have my own child." Rui-a explained her frame of mind and her decisions.

"Whether to have a child or not is an important issue, you really should discuss it with me." Young-tae's voice began to sound rather cold, his despondent demeanour suggested he had suffered a disastrous defeat.

"You were in prison, your heart was like being shackled with a heavy iron ball, I just can't bear to burden and confuse you any further." Rui-a fought back her tears and stood her ground firmly. She recalled the first time she visited the prison, it was painful for her to see a haggard and dispirited Young-tae.

Young-tae did not pursue the subject as he felt emotionally drained after the revelation. He felt as if a forceful whirlwind had lifted him high up in the air and then threw him mercilessly onto the ground with a heavy thud.

"Rui-a, it's getting late, there are still a lot of things to do at home." Mdm Shim asked for Rui-a to make a move while she and little Taek stood next to the white sedan.

"Little Taek, tomorrow we will go for a medical check-up in the hospital and after that we go buy some toys, okay?" When they returned to the car, Rui-a asked her son. "Okay, mommy." Replied Little Taek.

"Little Taek, can I hold you?" Even though he had not gotten his assurance, Young-tae thought Rui-a would not lie to him. He lifted little Taek and looked at his facial feature for resemblance.

Then he asked, "Little Taek, do you like to eat chocolate?"

"No, I hate chocolate." Replied the little boy with a sneer.

"How about drinks, do you like to drink soda?" Asked Young-tae as he tried to find out little Taek's dieting habit for a purpose. "No, I hate soda." Again, little Taek replied with a sneer.

"Okay, I'll buy you some toys tomorrow." Young-tae said that to please him.

The answers from little Taek were assurance to him as chocolate and soda were exactly the two things Young-tae disliked since he was a kid.

He then held little Taek closely, he felt he had let him down for so many years and felt sorry for not being able to provide him with a credible father figure. On the way to his new house, tears streamed incessantly down his cheeks while holding little Taek in his arms.

A New Beginning

The vehicle headed north of Seoul. Rui-a bought a house in Dobong district as she thought Young-tae would feel more comfortable living in a place with mountains and greenery in the surrounding.

The car came to a stop at the front porch of a private house, little Taek had been sleeping and resting his head on Young-tae's shoulder. He carried him to the house without waking him up.

"How can we afford such a costly private house?" Young-tae was bemused.

"It's your money, the paintings you painted while in prison fetched really good money." Said Rui-a.

"Show me the revenue from selling my paintings later." Young-tae was curious how much he had earned from selling his paintings, but he was occupied with little Taek.

Mdm Shim went to the kitchen to get the dinner ready. Dinner was earnestly prepared since that morning, before they went to fetch Young-tae. They had just moved to this new house one month ago, since then, she was delighted and in good spirit as the house was bright and spacious, and the neighbourhood was peaceful and safe. She was especially fond of the local markets where a wide variety of fresh local produce and delicacies were available.

Young-tae was still carrying little Taek while Rui-a showed him around the house. There was a study room, two bedrooms, a living room, a kitchen, as well as a painting studio. Young-tae thought Rui-a should not spend so much money on a house, but was touched by her dedication to build a comfortable home for him.

"You did a good job, thank you." Young-tae showed his appreciation as he saw the painting studio Rui-a had set up for him.

"I'm glad you are okay with it. I bought some clothes and underwear for you, they are in the master bedroom." Replied Rui-a, she was relieved to hear a positive comment from Young-tae.

"That's fine. Thank you." Replied Young-tae.

"Come, we have to wake little Taek up for dinner, put him down on the sofa." Said Rui-a as she went to the kitchen to help set up dinner.

Dinner was sumptuous and cordial, it had been a long time since Young-tae tasted Mdm Shim's home-made dishes.

"Auntie, I really enjoyed the dinner, thank you for preparing my favourite food." Young-tae was genuinely touched by the two magnanimous souls who had arranged such a heart-warming homecoming for him.

After dinner, Young-tae thought he should express his remorse to Mdm Shim formally. They were in the study room, Mdm Shim was seated on the floor, and Young-tae kneeled before her, Rui-a came to join them after tucking little Taek in bed.

"Auntie, please forgive me. I've done serious mistakes in the past that had hurt you, Rui-a and Joo-a. Please forgive me." There were too much pent up emotions in him, Young-tae began to sob as he asked for forgiveness.

"My poor child. Your mistakes really hurt us, but we've decided to leave the past behind and not let it haunt us in future. I understand Eun-ja's death had traumatized you up to the extent that you closed your heart and kept everything to yourself. For a long time, we thought you were doing fine. It was partly our fault for not being able to really connect with you. Sometimes heaven is cruel, we can only accept the reality and carry on with our lives. We really need you at home, little Taek needs a father. Together, we must do a good job in bringing him up." Mdm Shim empathized with Young-tae and had forgiven his past errant behaviour.

The atmosphere was sombre, the more forgiving Mdm Shim was, the more it hurt Young-tae's heart.

"I'm really ashamed of myself, how I wish I could just vanish into thin air! How am I supposed to be little Taek's father, I'm not qualified! Ahh…my heart is really painful…" Young-tae began to cry convulsively as he revealed his innermost fear in front of the two women.

"My poor child!" Mdm Shim started sobbing as she felt the agonizing pain in Young-tae's soul. Rui-a was affected and started weeping too. Both of them could not find any comforting words to console him.

After Eun-ja passed away, Young-tae hardly mentioned about the pain of losing her, only until now he was able to release all his pain by crying his heart out. The prospect of getting a new lease of life offered a pretext for unloading his emotional baggage.

Three months later, the family took a trip to Nami Island. Young-tae set up his easel near the riverbank. Mdm Shim laid a picnic mat on the ground next to Young-tae, while Rui-a took out some snacks and refreshment from the picnic basket. Little Taek was pestering his father to teach him painting. Young-tae held his son in one hand and started teaching him the correct way to hold a painting brush.

Autumn at Nami Island was colourful, with yellow, orange and red leaves on the tall trees all over the island. Young-tae's mind was as clear as the sky, as he was certain that the islands would remain where they are and would embrace him unconditionally.

THE END

REFERENCES

1. http://crime.about.com/odserial/a/psychopaths.htm
   Title: Characteristics of the Psychopathic Personality -
   Psychopathic Behavior
   Author: Charles Montaldo

2. http://psychopathyawareness.wordpress.com/
   2011/10/03/the-list-of-psychopathy-symptoms/
   Title: The List of Psychopathy Symptoms: Hervery
   Cleckley and Robert Harer
   Author: Claudia Moscovici

3. http://webmagazine.maastrichtuniversity.
   nl/index.php/research/mind/
   item/355-some-psychopaths-can-be-treated
   Title: Some psychopaths can be treated (David
   Bernstein)
   Author: Hans van Vinkeveen

4. http://www.psychiatrictimes.com/psychotic-
   affective-disorders/hidden-suffering-psychopath-0
   Title: The Hidden Suffering of the Psychopath
   Author: Willem H.J. Martens

5. http://www.lovefraud.com/2008/07/25/
   medication-used-to-treat-sociopathypsychopathy/
   Title: Medication used to treat sociopathy/psychopathy
   Author: Liane Leedom

6. http://www.diffen.com/difference/Psychopath_vs_Sociopath
    Title: Psychopath vs Sociopath
    Author: Diffen

7. https://translate.google.com/

8. http://www.calmdownmind.com/seeing-through-deluded-thinking/
    Title: Seeing Through Deluded Thinking
    Author: Sen

9. http://english.visitkorea.or.kr/enu/
    Title: Visit Korea
    By Korea Tourism Organization

10. Simon Richmond, Yu-Mei Balasingamchow, Cesar G Soriano, Rob Whyte
    Title: Korea (8th Edition, 2010)
    Publisher: Lonely Planet

11. Simon Richmond, Timothy N Hornyak, Shawn Low
    Title: Korea (9th Edition, 2013)
    Publisher: Lonely Planet

12. Cecilla Hae-Jin Lee
    Title: Frommer's South Korea (2nd Edition, 2010)
    Publisher: Wiley Publishing, Inc.

13. Catherine Collin, Voula Grand, Nigel Benson, Merrrin Lazyan, Joannah Ginsburg, Marcus Weeks
    Title: The Psychology Book (2011)
    Publisher: Dorling Kindersley Ltd (Penguin Group, UK)

14. Laurence Gonzales
    Title: Suriving Survival - The art and science of resilience (2013)
    Publisher: W.W. Norton & Company Ltd
15. Suzanne Redfern and Susan K. Gilbert
    Title: The Grieving Garden - Living with the Death of a Child
    Publisher: Hampton Roads Publishing Company, Inc.